AUTOMAT

Stephanie Kane

COLD HARD PRESS
Denver, Colorado

A Perfect Eye
A Denver Post Bestseller

"An artistic thriller that will keep readers guessing and please the author's fans."

—Kirkus Reviews

"Come for the setting, stay for the story. An absorbing mystery set in familiar territory. A bonus: you learn an awful lot about art restoration."

—The Denver Post

"This is really one of those books you can't put down. It is both an enlightening and wonderfully told inside story of the world of art curators and forgeries and a gripping thriller. You wonder why you didn't see the ending coming, which is truly the mark of a compelling and skillfully told mystery."

—Harry Maclean, Edgar Award Winner and #1 New York Times Bestselling Author of *In Broad Daylight*

"Lily Sparks' keen powers of observation and Stephanie Kane's snappy, hard-edged writing make for a highly original mystery that provides a whole gallery full of heart-pounding chills."

—Mark Stevens, Author of the Allison Coil Mystery Series including *The Melancholy Howl*

"A great mystery story that is page-turning. I loved the story and actually finished it in a few hours."

—Celtic Lady's Reviews

"The story is full of intrigue and draws you in. A good murder from beginning to end."

—Hello Booklover

Seeds of Doubt
Colorado Authors League Award Winner

"Kane deserves to join the ranks of the big-time legal-thriller eagles."
—Publishers Weekly

"Kane's background as a defense attorney informs the legal thriller backbone of the story, but the exploration of childhood sins, whether monstrous or incidental, gives *Seeds of Doubt* its emotional heft."
—The Baltimore Sun

"Deftly written."

—Chicago Sun

"One of the outstanding mysteries of the year."
—The Cleveland Plain-Dealer

Extreme Indifference
Colorado Book Award Winner
Colorado Authors League Award Winner

"Sturdy intrigue in and out of court with an especially sharp eye for the riptides of power running just beneath the legal quiddities."
—Kirkus Reviews

"Fast-moving and intriguing. Kane knows both her protagonist and the legal terrain well."
—San Francisco Chronicle

"A tight, well-written thriller with an ending that caught me completely off-balance."
—The Cleveland Plain-Dealer

Blind Spot

Quiet Time

"Stephanie Kane does it again. *Quiet Time* keeps your mind thinking and your heart racing – What a great read!"

—Rikki Klieman, Court TV

"Life's greatest dramas play out in family life. And never have those passions more relentlessly imprinted on generation after generation than when they enfold in a vacuum of secrecy.... The end is riveting and a surprise—but that's what Kane is all about."

—*The Denver Post*

"An atmospheric gothic-like work of suspense that imbues the reader with the feeling that something is going to happen very soon. Stephanie Kane is a terrific storyteller who knows how to grab the attention of the audience and keeps it."

——*The Midwest Book Review*

"Kane's work is just as good as the trial mysteries written by Steve Martini."

—*The Drood Review of Mystery*

"Kane weaves an intricate story. Her prose is refreshing and light."

——I Love A Mystery

Also by Stephanie Kane

AUTOMAT

First Edition
First Printing, 2020

Cold Hard Press
Denver, CO

Book interior design by Susan Brooks
Cover design by Marcel Venter

Library of Congress Number: 2020908544

ISBN Print: 978-1-7336715-4-5
ISBN Digital: 978-1-7336715-5-2

Printed in the United States of America

In memory of my sister, Uma

Chapter One

Offbeat Theater was standing room only this hot June night. In the mezzanine, Denver's glitterati fanned themselves with their programs, sending patchouli and old money up to the balcony where Lily Sparks, The Denver Art Museum's Conservator of Paintings, was taking her seat. She helped her mentor, Elena Brandt, remove her cape.

"Nervous, dear?" Elena asked.

"Yup." She couldn't wait for this dog-and-pony show to end.

"You've done the hard work." Elena patted her hand. "It's all over but the shouting."

Lily popped an Advil.

Down below, the theater's artistic director Laird Bennett bounded to the stage. His hair was slicked back in a ponytail and sweat ringed the armpits of his paisley shirt.

"Is the Governor here?" he said.

The audience tittered indulgently.

"I hope we're not waiting for that jackass," Elena muttered loudly. A man below them glanced up, but Brandt Fine Art's proprietress could get away with it.

"There's an open bar later," Lily assured her.

"Thank God it's one act."

This patrons-only event kicked off the countdown to the museum's blockbuster Edward Hopper show. Museums could no longer afford to be tombs to dead artists; now they had to entertain and provoke. In a nod to shrinking attention spans, the museum had commissioned Offbeat to promote the exhibition with tonight's burst of micro-theater. When the swamp cooler finally subsided, Bennett launched in.

"Offbeat Theater and The Denver Art Museum welcome you to a very special performance." He saluted museum director Michel Roland in the opposite balcony. Sitting with Angela Kurtz, head of The Kurtz Foundation and chairwoman of his Board of Trustees, Michel stiffly nodded back. "For nearly a century, viewers have debated what the lonely young flapper in Edward Hopper's *Automat* was thinking as she gazed into her coffee cup. Tonight, when she steps out of the painting and onto the stage, she'll tell you herself."

The curtain parted. A spotlight lit a pedestal table where the flapper, in felt cloche, leather gloves and fur-trimmed coat, stared into a diner cup.

Bennett moved to the wings. "What runs through her mind?" he mused. "A faithless lover, her next meal, or—"

"What idiot made her wear gloves and fur in this heat!" Elena called out.

"—does she yearn for something more?"

As the opening bars of *Misty* played, the flapper raised her cup.

Bennett slipped into the seat next to Lily's, suffusing the balcony with the smell of wine and sweat. On stage the girl coyly extended her leg. A strappy sandal caught the light. Its toe caressed the other leg like a kitten wanting to be fed.

A finger at a time, the girl stripped off one glove, then the other. Bennett gripped the balcony's rail. Two women in the audience bent their heads together and whispered but were quickly shushed.

Off came the girl's cloche. Blonde hair tumbled down. Defiantly she raised her chin. Her kohl-rimmed eyes burned. She rose and faced the audience with a magnificent contempt.

The stage's back wall lit red.

The girl tore off her coat.

The audience gasped.

A spotlight played across her jutting chin, torpedo breasts and muscular thighs. She froze and her sandals flashed. Nude, she strode across the stage like Caesar before the Gauls. A cymbal clashed and she struck a pose. A man in the front row clapped. A woman hesitantly joined in. The applause turned to a drumbeat and whoops, and Michel led a standing ovation.

"That's not what I imagined Hopper's girl was thinking." Lily gathered Elena's cape and helped her up. "And those shoes weren't in *Automat*."

"Her fuck-me's?" Elena smiled wickedly. "Now where's my drink?"

Patrons mobbed Michel and his entourage in the lobby. Cutting them a wide berth, Lily got Elena a glass of champagne and a cherry tartlet on a diner plate. The quicker they left, the better. For the past six months she'd been on a whirlwind tour around the country with Angela Kurtz assembling Hoppers for the show, and first thing in the morning movers would be at her conservation lab to start transporting them to the exhibition gallery.

"Where's Bennett?" she asked Elena. The sweaty artistic director had disappeared.

"Getting his kudos backstage." Elena sniffed. "He and Cam should be ashamed."

"Cam?"

"Maddox. The so-called playwright." Elena gestured at a portly man with a walrus moustache who was chatting up the critic from the alt weekly. A kid dressed in black hovered at their side. "Let's get out—"

A man next to them made a grand gesture. Lily saw his glass of Cabernet coming her way the moment before it hit. She looked down at the bodice of her new dress. A dark red stain was spreading across its soft white folds. The guy was already disappearing into the crowd. A fitting ending to this lousy evening. "Damn! I'll never get this out!"

"Dab it with club soda," Elena said.

Patrons were three-deep at the bar. Where was the powder room? Coat check, box office… Under the stairs to the balcony was an unmarked door.

"I'll be right back," she told Elena.

Lily made her way to the door and knocked.

"Hello?"

No answer. She rattled the knob.

The door opened onto an alcove. A halogen spot lit a small table where the flapper, back in her cloche and coat, hunched over her cup. Behind her was a mirror.

"Oh, sorry!" Lily said. "I was looking for the powder room."

The flapper stared into her cup. Close up, she seemed older than she'd appeared onstage. Her gloved hands rested between the cup and snack plate. Vamping under those hot lights must have been exhausting; was she taking a break before a private after-party? The plate had no fork or crumbs; the lobby's refreshments must not have made their way in here. And what was she doing in that sweltering coat?

"Can you point me to the ladies?" Lily asked.

A curl peeked from under the cloche. There was a bead of moisture at the tip.

"Miss—"

The halogen made the fur on the flapper's collar squirm. A familiar odor wafted up, musty and metallic. Lily touched the girl's shoulder. Her hand came away wet. The drop from the curl hit the snack plate. Ruby red. She grabbed her chin and the cloche fell away.

The flapper's face was gray. Her eyes were coals, her flaccid lips the color of a bruise. Even her hair was lifeless, the gold faded to ash. But her collar was alive. Saturated, the fur pulsed and dripped. Red ran from the tips of the bristles down the sleeve and into the cup.

This couldn't be happening again.

Lily dropped the girl's chin, her own fingers tingling from its rubbery flesh. A look at her face confirmed the flapper was no ingenue—early thirties, at least. She closed her eyes, willing the dead woman away. But another image came, one she'd been trying to forget for the better part of a year. Angela Kurtz's father, George, in the library of his Country Club mansion, his intestines smeared into the celadon-and-gold-leaf wallpaper. She alone had recognized that horror for what it was: a man rendered into an Impressionist painting, the ultimate defiling of humanity and art ....

A burst of laughter came from the lobby.

Lily's eyes jerked open. The flapper was still there. She had a gift. Did she owe it to this poor woman to use it?

She closed the door behind her and latched it.

Steeling herself, she gently raised the flapper's chin again. A black gash below her ear raced to a viscous hole in her throat, then caromed to the other ear. Skin curled protectively around the hole, trying to close it. Lily's hand jerked and the dead woman's head dropped all the way back. The hole gaped like a mouth with jagged teeth.

More laughter came from outside. Louder, closer. She had a minute or two at most.... Art into murder. Was this a crime of opportunity, or was the killer trying to recreate Hopper's painting and kill the girl in it? Picturing the painting, she stepped back.

In *Automat*, a glass window reflected the automat's cold lights and emptiness; here the mirror amplified the queasy intimacy of the solitary figure hunched over her cup. Cup, saucer, snack plate—but in the painting there was an object between the girl and the window, a pop of color on the ledge. A bowl of fruit? The coat and cloche seemed right, but something was off with the gloves. Did Hopper's girl wear two—or just one? Time ticked and her mind raced.

Canvases were two-dimensional and cropped. Hopper's *Automat* cut off his girl at the legs. Lily peered under the table. The flapper still wore fuck-me's, but were they the same ones she'd pranced across the stage in? The straps cut into her ankles and her feet were jammed into the toe box.

Lily rose and carefully repositioned the flapper's head to lean over the coffee cup. She returned the cloche to her dulled hair.

Now other eyes could look.

Chapter Two

"Morbid, are we?" Matt said.

Lily clicked out of her computer. She'd been right about the glove. There was just one in Hopper's *Automat*, on the flapper's hand by the snack plate. And a crystal bowl of apples, bananas and oranges sat on the plate-glass window's ledge. If the killer was recreating the painting, he'd missed a couple of details. She turned to her assistant.

"What was she thinking, Matt?"

"The dead girl?" Matt rolled his eyes. Though his hornrims and button-down shirts made him look like a nerdy Clark Kent, over the past year he'd loosened up enough to crack an occasional joke. Now he was at a loss, not that she could blame him.

She'd spent half the night being grilled by cops, only to arrive at the lab to a fresh barrage from her colleagues. Yes, it was ghastly. No, I didn't meet her. And there's nothing quite like a murder to make an exhibition a success! There'd be no show now; Michel's e-mail about an all-hands-on-deck meeting in ten minutes made its fate clear. Apparently nobody had clued in the art handlers, because one of them—James—was here to transport *Couple near Poplars*, Hopper's 1906 watercolor of a petite

Gibson girl and her swain, to the exhibition gallery. Its lender would undoubtedly pull the plug, but there was still time for one last teachable moment for Matt.

"What do you see?" she asked him.

"Uh—she's not that into him?" James said.

Lily glanced up. Like good handlers, James tended to fade into the woodwork. Handlers had to get along with everyone from curators to mount-makers to artists, and James's receding hairline and comfortable paunch made it easy to overlook the training the job required. But she hadn't expected him to chime in.

"Why do you say that?" she asked.

"Well, they're together… but not."

Hopper had painted *Couple* on his first trip to Paris. The girl with upswept hair and a pinafore over her corseted waist stood with a beanstalk of a man with a beret and a pencil moustache. Both stared into the distance; what could have been an intimate glimpse of a young couple in love was inexplicably grim. But Matt and James were more interested in the Objects Conservator's slender young assistant sashaying past in skintight jeans and leopard-print mules.

"Beguiling," Matt muttered.

James nodded. Then, as if he suddenly remembered why he was there, he reached for the painting.

"Can you just give us a couple of minutes with this?" Lily asked him. She pointed to the tiny cluster of spidery stains in *Couple*'s upper corner. "The foxing, Matt."

"Oh, yeah. It's in your condition report."

Her cross-country trip with Angela Kurtz to procure the Hoppers hadn't been all fancy dinners with curators from The Whitney and The Met. Besides certifying the paintings were stable enough to travel, she'd had to document their condition before and after they arrived at the museum. But even before the murder, something about Hopper's work had made her uneasy. The women in his paintings never met your eyes.

"Must be hard to let it go," James said. "I mean from the lab."

Maybe it wasn't the women, but Hopper's lighting. It was cold, and even when it streamed through a window, it was hard to determine its source. You couldn't tell the time of day, or even the year. Take *Couple*. The sky was beige but the hill in the background was brightly lit. By the sun, or was it the vegetation changing color? The poplars bent in the wind, but Gibson Girl's pinafore didn't move. Were Hopper's mixed messages intended to throw the viewer off balance? But this was Matt's last moment with the rare watercolor.

"The beret," Lily prompted him. "What about the pigment?"

"The cobalt hasn't faded one bit."

"And the girl?"

"Just a hint of rouge."

That brought Lily back to earth.

Except for the black ribbon at her throat, Gibson Girl looked nothing like the dead actress whom the morning *Post* had identified as Vanessa Randall. Offbeat lamented the loss of a luminous talent and cherished member of its troupe, sentiments undercut by artistic director Laird Bennett's mention of an understudy.

"You'll be late," a voice behind them said.

The lab's overhead lights made Dr. Gina Wheelock's silver Mohawk flash. The Curator of Paintings was easy to pimp; Lily ran her fingers through her own shoulder-length honey-blonde hair, and Gina's hand reflexively rose but stopped just in time to convert the gesture to a pat. Mousse intact, she fixed Lily with a rabid smile. "Have fun gallivanting around the country with Angela?"

"I love writing condition reports." Lily knew Gina was still smarting over Angela not taking her on the tour. "But too bad Michel's pulling the plug. There go your flash mobs."

Gina flushed. She'd sold Michel on bringing *Automat* to the stage as a daring innovation on tableaux vivants, those silent actors who posed like statues in public squares throughout Europe. Michel could bring a touch of Paris to Denver before next year's Coco Chanel show! Flush with her success at convincing him, Gina had commissioned Offbeat to bring three more Hoppers to life in public locations before the gala, tweeting them out at the last minute to the museum's mailing list to generate a flash-mob response. Now all that would be scrapped.

"Maybe he'll change his mind," Gina said.

"Michel? No way."

"Want to bet?" Gina turned to the art handler. "What are you gawking at, Jamie?"

"James."

"Whatever." Gina pointed to *Couple*. "Aren't you here to courier this painting to the gallery? Where are your gloves?"

"Right here, Dr. Wheelock." Glancing slyly at Lily, James put them on. It was an open secret that she never wore gloves either; cotton was slippery and misjudging your grip in the lab could be fatal. "Okay if I take it now, Ms. Sparks?"

"Coming?" Gina cooed at Lily.

"I'll meet you there."

Lily looked at *Couple* again.

James was right: Gibson Girl wasn't into Beret Man. He was trying to draw her closer, but she recoiled from his touch. Her lips were set, her arms folded tightly across her chest, her trim leather boots pointed resolutely away from his. Beret Man felt it too. His spidery clutch was uncertain, his pinky loose. His expression— maybe his hands—reminded her of Laird Bennett watching Vanessa Randall strut the stage.

Chapter Three

Lily was the last to arrive at Michel's meeting. He liked meetings but not crowds, and as always, his control was on display. His chandelier overhung an oval conference table with seven leather swivel chairs, five of them already occupied. The one at the de facto head of the table was elevated. Lily slipped into the last low chair and Michel took the high one.

"Coffee?" he said.

The chandelier glinted off a silver service on the sideboard, but there were no takers. Pinched expressions and jiggling knees said his top administrative dogs had already tanked up.

"Croissants?" he offered. The pastries were in the center of the table, out of reach.

Wendy, his COO, downed a Tums.

Michel squared his sloping shoulders. He gestured to his executive assistant, who usually sat behind him with a notepad, to leave and close the door behind her. He steepled his fingers and gazed at each of them in turn. "The gala is in exactly two weeks," he said. "Does the show go on?"

Nobody answered.

He nodded genially at his CFO. "We'll start with Stu."

"Um…" Stu took off his glasses and rubbed his eyes.

Poor Stu. Museums everywhere were dealing with aging memberships and plunging ticket sales, and Michel wasn't the only director to depend on blockbusters to make the nut. But blockbusters were like crack. The high never lasted and each time it took more.

Michel showed his teeth. "Come now, Stu, you're among friends."

"We have to keep our eye on the bigger prize, Michel," Stu said. Not to mention the exhibition catalog whose hard and softback editions were in second printings, and the truckload of faux felt cloches and diner mugs at the loading dock that morning when Lily badged in.

Michel leaned forward. "Meaning?"

"We're competing with The Zoo and The Botanic Gardens for SCFD funds," Stu said. The municipal pot of gold that overflowed with tax revenues from legalized pot. "Public speculation on the museum's connection to a murder—"

"Shall I take that as a no?"

Lily closed her eyes and pictured the crime scene. Cup, saucer, snack plate—a mirror instead of *Automat's* glass window, two gloves, no bowl of fruit. Crazy to think the killer was recreating the painting, much less deliberately introducing mistakes to throw the viewer off. Vanessa Randall was murdered in a theater, and there was nothing unique about any of those props. Maybe the alcove was just a storage room with a table and a mirror, where she'd gone to escape the crowd. But why was she wearing that sweltering coat?

"Are we boring you, Ms. Sparks?" Michel said. "Or perhaps you need to catch up on your sleep."

Her eyes jerked open. Across the table Kip, the museum's burly mount-maker, grinned at her. He reached for a chocolate croissant, making the chandelier sway and distracting Michel. Kip was never invited to these meetings; he made unwieldy pieces of art float, not administrative decisions. Michel curated his meetings, and he loved titles. But the mount-maker had neither a title nor an acronym. Did

Michel summon Kip just to fill the seventh chair? COO Wendy popped another Tums.

Michel swiveled in her direction. "Wendy?"

"What if someone poisons the food and drink? We'll need more security at the gala."

Michel frowned. Would she use the L-words?

Wendy bravely forged on. "Not to mention off-site Liability for the tableaux. We should call Legal—"

"No! Pru?"

Poor Pru. The CMO's mission was to avoid controversy and preserve the museum's rep.

She cleared her throat. "A full-time employee already handles our relationship with the city, Michel. Out-of-towners drawn by the blockbuster will be a nightmare."

Michel leaned back. Even the chandelier was silent.

Poor Michel. Nobody had the guts to tell him to cancel, but it was three to nothing against his show and he'd take it personally.

Michel disdained Americans but loved Americana. Hopper's settings were gas stations and diners and hotel lobbies, but like cowboys, his subjects were quintessentially alone. Which actually made Hopper— *French*, right up there with "le Clint", film noir, and *qu'est-ce que le bonheur*. But Michel's stake in the show transcended his cultural DNA, the existential dilemma of the meaning of happiness, even his need to compete with The Museum of Contemporary Arts. After Denver, Hopper was going on the road. Michel would leverage the chits from its cross-country tour to vault himself back onto the international stage. If he got cover.

Michel's ferrety gaze roamed the table. Lily pictured the crime scene again. If—*if*—the killer was trying to recreate *Automat*, why the fuck-me's and two gloves?

"And you, Gina?" he said.

The Curator of Paintings' mission was to care for the museum's art, a fitting role for a COP. Gina squared her shoulders. "Nobody's more committed to Hopper than me, Michel, but there's simply no reason to connect an actress's death to us or the show. What will the public think if we postpone? Wouldn't that be admitting—"

"Cancel," Lily said.

Kip stopped mid-bite. The others swiveled towards her.

"What?" Michel said.

"Vanessa Randall's dead," Lily said, "and her killer's out there."

Michel and Gina exchanged a glance.

"Bravo, Ms Sparks!" He clapped his hands. "Another star turn at the museum's expense."

"I beg your pardon?"

Gina jumped in. "That's why Angela took you on tour, isn't it? Catching her father's killer made you queen for the day! How like you to see a murder wherever you look."

Lily held her temper. "But Vanessa Randall was—"

"And you're the one to solve it." Michel nodded knowingly. "Where would we be if you hadn't caught George's murder? Why, not even the Denver Police Department—"

"Where will we be if he kills again, Michel?" Lily asked.

"You care nothing about this museum—"

The door flung open.

"Angela!" Michel cried. "So good of you—"

"If only you'd told me when."

Angela Kurtz had come a long way in the year since her father died. With her hair chicly streaked, in her silk designer sheath and elegant stilettos with pointy toes and slender straps, she wasn't just head of The Kurtz Foundation and chairwoman of Michel's board of trustees. She could yank the exhibition right out from under his feet.

Angela smiled tightly. "Shall I pull up a chair?"

"Kip—" Michel began.

"You stay right there!" she ordered.

As Angela strode to the head of the table and plunked her Prada bag on the floor, the chandelier swayed. Michel retreated to his desk.

"Where were we?" Angela said.

"The young actress's tragic death—" he began.

"*Quel dommage* for you both." In museum-world, patrons reigned supreme, but nothing was worse than looking foolish. A murder could cause loans to be pulled. The exhibition had been assembled over six months and thousands of miles, and Angela's reputation was on the line. "What's your decision, Michel?"

He shrugged helplessly. "I am but a first among equals, Angela. In our little democracy, every member has a vote. We were just hearing from Ms. Sparks."

"Lily?" Angela asked.

Museums hung only a fraction of their art. Angela didn't just know the real treasures, she knew where they were buried. Curators never spoke of the off-site climate-controlled concrete facilities with state-of-the-art fire detectors that rang before there was smoke and cut off the sprinklers before they damaged the art. They guarded those fortresses' addresses with their lives.

"Lily?" Angela repeated.

Watch how it's done, she'd told Lily. Over martinis at a place so tiny and impossible to get into it didn't have a name, she'd stuck it to the curator of The Met. *Show us the good stuff.* The next day they'd toured The Met's fortress, as anonymous from the outside as it was spectacular within. Cézannes, Monets, Picassos, an Old Master—in mint condition, stored vertically like one-of-a-kind gowns in the world's most exclusive bridal boutique. *We don't want what's on your walls*, Angela had said, *we want what's in your vault....*

Michel was looking at Lily. "Mademoiselle?"

What she said next could determine her future not just with the museum, but with Angela. Lily took a deep breath.

"Cancel the show. With a killer out there, it's too big a risk."

Angela sighed, then slowly nodded. "Point taken." She was no stranger to violent death; more than that, she respected the power of vengeance. But she wasn't her father's daughter for nothing. She turned briskly to Michel. "None of the Hoppers are at risk and canceling won't catch the killer. Beef up security."

Michel recovered swiftly. "My thoughts exactly!"

"*Vive le roi*," Angela said drily.

He smiled modestly. "George would be so proud—"

Angela cut him off. "Indeed."

Michel nodded. "And we'll leave that… nasty business of that poor actress to the authorities."

Kip snagged another croissant and Angela reached for her bag. Barely concealing their relief, Gina and the rest of the staff filed out. Michel motioned Lily to stay. His bonhomie had evaporated with the crowd.

"If I hear one word about you investigating this," he said, "you're fired."

———

"What did Michel want?" Gina asked outside.

"An update on a condition report."

"I'll bet." Gina scrolled her phone. "But you're lucky he didn't cancel."

"Yeah?"

"They nabbed Vanessa Randall's killer."

"Who?"

"Andy Bragg, a trainer she dated at the DAC." The swank downtown athletic club. "An ex in a testosterone-fueled rage. Ask your FBI man about those."

Lily ignored the jab; Gina's grudges were epic. Instead she pictured Vanessa Randall. Blood dripping from collar to cup. No splatter or stab wound; it almost looked like her killer had attacked her from behind. Testosterone-fueled rage?

If it was Vanessa's ex-boyfriend, he'd want her to see it coming.

Chapter Four

Forty years of rising before dawn to deliver the U.S. mail had made Lily's dad perpetually early; retirement had left him with insomnia and nothing to get up for. In the dining room of an imposing brick tower near the Country Club, at his usual table with his back to the wall and pretending to study the menu, he waited now. With three minutes to spare, Lily hurried across the floor and kissed his cheek. Was that cologne?

"Waiting long, Dad?" she said.

"You're worth it, Lily."

In khakis and a pressed shirt, he sat ramrod straight with his bad leg tucked neatly under his chair. Despite the aftershave he looked grayer, in a fog. He gave Lily the menu. She'd memorized it, too: London Broil au jus, tilapia with salsa, vegetarian meatloaf. He hated meatloaf.

"What's good tonight?" she said.

"Without salt it's all the same."

At their old bungalow she'd brought him takeout from Boston Market. Now dinner was a way to use up his mandatory meal tickets. She ordered the tilapia.

"What's new, honey?" He'd stopped reading *The Post.*

"Nothing, really."

"When does your show open?" he asked.

"Two weeks." But he didn't care about Hopper.

To her dad, art was artifice and painters were tricksters who made reality appear something it was not. Truth, on the other hand, could be counted, weighed and delivered like a sack of mail. But her travels with Angela had made him proud: she was moving up in the world.

"And your FBI friend—Paul?" Points for asking, but he choked on the name.

"He's up for a promotion, Dad."

"In D.C.?"

"Yeah." That should cheer him up.

"Good."

Despite the early hour, the tables were filled. This dining room was straight out of a Hopper—not even the couple across the floor talked. The hush of supping soup was broken only by the jingle of silverware.

"Here you go, Harry." The waitress set down their plates and winked at him like they were old friends.

"Dig in," he told Lily sardonically.

The tilapia was dry. White cloths and bread plates kicked the dining room's décor up a notch, but the silence reminded her of dinners when she was a kid. If her mom was with him here, would they talk? She set down her fork. "Something did happen."

His eyes lit. "Another murder?"

"An actress." Screw the London broil, this is what he hungered for.

"Details, please."

She filled him in on the crime scene and *Automat.*

"You think the killer has some 'in' with the artist, Lily?"

"Yes."

"But he got the details wrong."

To Dad, that's what counted. But maybe what the killer got right mattered more. She looked again at the couple across the floor. As in a Hopper, light streamed through the window behind them. Unlike a Hopper, it actually fell on the tablecloth and haloed the woman's white hair. If the killer was trying to recreate *Automat*, the window was important enough to him to replicate it with a mirror. Did he want to see himself?

"Steak okay, Harry?" The waitress hovered with a pitcher and basket of rolls.

"Delicious."

She beamed. "Eat up, now." She refilled their glasses and left.

The salsa tasted like tin, and Lily reached for a roll. Her bread plate was the size of the snack plate in *Automat*. The killer had gotten that detail right, too. The window in the painting reflected the automat's cold white lights, which meant it was nighttime. The flapper's stylish hat and coat suggested she'd stopped by for a snack after work. By including the mirror and snack plate, the killer had recreated something essential: the intimacy of a Depression Era shop girl's solitude. He didn't just try to replicate *Automat*; he respected Hopper.

"The effect, Dad. He got what the painting was about."

"Eat up."

She ate another morsel of fish, and he sawed at his steak. Who was kidding whom? This wasn't a Hopper, or even a real restaurant. It was the chow hall in an old-age home where dinner was at 4:00 and the cutlery lacked teeth. Swallowing her frustration, she looked at the elderly couple again. Still not speaking, they'd moved to dessert. She thought again of the long silences at the dinner table in her parents' bungalow. Did they ever love each other at all? But there were other ways to show love, like that time at JC Penney's right before her mom died.

It had been late winter, and flannel sheets were on sale. Clutching a set of blue ones, Mom marched past the shoes towards the check-out counter. On the way, they passed through lingerie. Mom couldn't help herself; she gave Lily the sheets to hold and pulled a dressing gown from the rack. It was white and strewn with nosegays of forget-me-nots. She stroked the silky lapel. Shaking her head, she returned it to the rack.

At the cash registers, Lily's breath caught. At eye level was a fairy-tale princess in a windowed box, in a satin dress and opera gloves. She'd never had a doll like that, had never seen anything so miraculous before. She wanted it so badly she trembled. *Mom…* Mom took her wallet from her purse and carefully counted out the money for the sheets. They drove home in silence. Lily knew she couldn't have the doll. It would have been wrong even to ask.

"Don't disappoint the waitress, honey," her dad was saying.

Ping—she ignored Gina's text.

The next morning, the JC Penney's princess had been at the foot of her bed. Two weeks later, Mom was dead. The last time Lily saw her, she'd been standing in the bungalow's doorway in her hat and coat, with a suitcase.

Ping. Gina again. Lily looked across the table at her dad.

After Mom died, he'd purged the bungalow of any trace of her. Too bad he missed the gold compact and that Polaroid of the gray-eyed blonde. *You'll age like your mother*, people always said, but how would Lily know? The woman in the Polaroid would never age, she'd always be an enigma. Paintings had secrets too. As paint aged and became transparent, preliminary sketches and alterations—pentimenti, the artist's regrets lurking in the canvas—emerged. Infrared showed damaged and retouched areas. X-raying Caravaggio's *Bacchus* revealed a painted-over self-portrait; hiding in a Jordaen was a woman's face under a cloud. But a marriage's secrets could be painted over forever.

"Dad—"

He was looking past her at a periwinkle-haired lady who was approaching with a determined look. "Harry!" she called.

"You're a sight for sore eyes, Doris," he said. She blinked suspiciously at Lily. "My daughter," he explained.

"Why, you work at the museum!" Doris said. She dropped her voice to a stage whisper. "That poor girl. They said it was the boyfriend. Too bad they let him go."

Lily looked at her phone. She should have read Gina's texts.

"An alibi," Doris said. "Five o'clock news."

Not Andy Bragg.

"Coming to the movie tonight, Harry?" Doris said. "There's popcorn…"

"I'll pick you up at six."

Doris winked at Lily and was off.

Dad rose like he was hefting a mailbag full of lead.

Remorse swept her. "You miss Mom?"

"She never left."

Chapter Five

"How's business, Elena?" Lily asked.

"Half my sales come from the Internet." This Saturday at noon the only traffic on Elena's block was a pair of yoga-togged thirty-somethings headed for True Food Kitchen, but in her cheetah caftan and genie slippers, Elena was chipper as ever. "Walk-ins like to kick the tires."

"And your show?" Urban flash mobs were a thing; Elena's exhibition of digital pix of them had drawn a rave review from *The Post*, but she was counting on Hopper to haul in out-of-towners.

Elena grimaced. "The selfie generation wants statement art."

"It's not always about making a sale," Lily reminded her.

"You're right, dear. It's about paying the rent." Elena put up the Closed sign and locked Brandt Fine Art's door. She never said no to lunch with Lily.

On the sidewalk, they circumvented a swath of construction netting. Elena's gallery was the only shop left on this block; the chic boutiques that had been her neighbors for thirty years were now excavation pits. Dodging orange cones, they waited at the corner for a Dodge RAM to pass. It hit a pothole and they reared back to avoid being splattered with mud. Lily grasped Elena's arm more firmly. When would she stop being too proud to use her walking stick?

"How do you stand this mess?" Lily said.

"On the weekend the wrecking ball stops." Behind her trademark, outsized red-framed glasses, Elena's eyes narrowed. "But you don't usually enter my war zone on Saturday. Michel's not canceling Hopper, is he?"

"Lord, no! The catering deposit's nonrefundable."

Elena laughed. "I don't suppose you had a say."

"We're a democracy. He took a vote."

Elena nodded approvingly. "Angela's a chip off the old block."

They crossed the street. This side had a hotel and a restaurant with outside seating for diners who didn't mind construction vehicles and dust.

"Ghastly business at the theater," Elena said. "Not getting involved, are you?"

"Of course not."

Luckily, Elena's favorite bistro was still standing. The waiter had no trouble seating them; they were the only customers. They ordered the lobster bisque.

"Speaking of the other night," Lily said, "it sounded like you know the playwright."

Elena swirled her Viognier. "Cam Maddox?"

"You said he should be ashamed."

Elena sniffed—at the wine or a memory? "Him and Laird Bennett."

"Tell me about them," Lily urged.

"Laird came from the Kennedy Center. He was Offbeat's big 'get.'"

"And?" Lily pushed.

"Like all directors, he likes ingenues."

But Vanessa was no ingenue. "Even after #MeToo?"

Elena laughed. "Men never think it applies to them."

The waiter brought their bisque with crackers instead of a baguette. Elena shook her head in dismay. She always looked forward to the baguette. "Speaking of automats, oh for the Horn & Hardart on Times Square!" she cried. "Chicken sandwiches and wedges of pie on diner plates, each behind a window waiting for a nickel or dime to drop. Like a strip joint on Forty-Second Street, you got what you paid for. No wonder Hopper painted it."

"You lost me, Elena."

She tsk-tsked. "Think of Amsterdam's red-light district, Lily, those scantily-clad bored-looking women behind glass. What are Hopper's paintings if not peepshows?"

It did make an odd sort of sense. Like the flapper in *Automat*, Hopper always framed his women with a window or door. If Vanessa's killer was a voyeur, maybe the mirror had more than one purpose. Which brought Lily back to the theater. "And Cam?" she asked. The mustachioed playwright.

Elena shrugged elaborately and crumbled the last cracker into her soup.

"He wrote the striptease," Lily prompted, "you said he should be ashamed too."

"What does your dashing FBI man think?"

The last thing Paul would want was her getting involved in another murder, and if Elena wasn't fooled about her interest in the crime, she'd never fool him. Since the news had broken yesterday, they'd been texting and playing phone tag. He was supposed to call tonight.

"I haven't asked."

Elena set down her spoon. "This cross-country affair of yours is bullshit."

"We're together, Elena. I go to D.C. or—"

"Not enough for a woman like you," Elena said, "or a man like him."

"We were talking about Cam Maddox."

"Ask Angela." Elena waved for the check, but Lily had prepaid it. Elena wagged her finger affectionately at her. "Back to the war zone. A deserter may want to kick tires."

Lily helped her to her feet. "Speaking of tires, want a lift to the museum Monday night? Sasha Lazar's giving the Hopper keynote."

"Wouldn't miss it for the world." Elena took Lily's arm. "Sasha knows all about peepshows."

Chapter Six

On her balcony overlooking the Botanic Garden, Lily waited for her swan. Moonlight made the Japanese pond fathomless, and shadows from ponderosa pines etched its glassy surface. A ripple broke from the pilings and widened in an arc. The swan glided out with its head under its wing. As it floated towards the island in the center of the pond, the moon lit its feathers like a torch.

Jack twitched.

"Don't even think about it," she warned.

His tail quivered.

"Remember last time?" George Kurtz's killer had broken into her condo and thrown Jack off the balcony. A snowdrift had saved him, but now it was spring and she didn't want to test how many lives he had left. The swan fanned its feathers, and Jack's sable haunches wagged.

The phone rang. Jack flicked his tail, jumped from her lap and sauntered inside.

"Lily?" It was Paul. Midnight in D.C.

"Working late?" She locked her balcony and went through the condo turning out lights.

"It's been hectic." His boss had been nominated to head the FBI, and Paul was testifying for him before the Senate next week. "But that's not why I called. Are you okay? I heard you found that girl's body."

So he'd been talking to his local contacts. Probably Johnson, that idiot who'd interviewed her at the police station Thursday night. "I'm fine, Paul. It has nothing to do with me or the museum."

"Didn't think it did." Ice clinked. "Let the cops handle it, honey."

By arresting the wrong guy and letting him go? Paul's voice, burred with whiskey and fatigue, made her miss him so badly she wished he were here right now. Maybe he—and God forbid, Gina and Michel!—were right. Let the cops handle it. He certainly had enough on his plate.

"How's the prep?" she asked.

"Piece of cake. Mark's as clean as they come." His nonchalance didn't fool her; the next confirmation hearing would be his for Assistant Director. Would he keep that studio apartment of his in D.C.? Instead of a Japanese garden, its balcony overlooked asphalt and cement.

"…same wife thirty years…"

Lulled by his voice, Lily climbed into bed. Jack curled up and began giving himself a bath. He and Paul were two of a kind; Jack's plush fur even smelled like cloves. Were museums hiring in D.C.? Conservators weren't exactly in demand, and she'd be starting at the bottom. But Elena was right. Murder aside, this was a helluva way to spend a Saturday night.

"…not even a parking ticket …"

She closed her eyes and pictured Paul coming out of the shower, short black Fed-style hair wet, towel at his waist. Sandalwood shaving cream, underneath it his own clove scent… She blinked away the livid scar on his chest. He'd canceled his last two trips to Denver. How long had it been? Not enough for a man like him—or a woman like her.

"…wasn't always a desk jockey," he was saying. "Mark has more commendations for bravery than you can count."

The scar flickered and they were back in that filthy shack with Dad and Kurtz's killer. Paul in his T-shirt and jeans, with nothing between him and a machete but the courage and wits that had given her time to grab Dad and run. When she came back for him, Paul was bleeding out on the dirt floor.

"Lily?"

The words tumbled out. "I want to come to your hearing."

"In D.C.?"

"Just for a couple of days."

"What about your show?" he said doubtfully.

"The gala's not till the end of next week." Her work on Hopper was done, and Gina and Michel would be glad she was gone.

"What's really going on?" Paul's drowsiness was fading.

She laughed lightly. "Can't a girl just pick up and—"

"You're not spontaneous, Lily. Impulsive, maybe—it's about the dead girl, right? Vanessa Randall." His glass slammed down with a thud. "Goddammit, are you in danger?"

"No!" Jack jumped down from the bed. "I just—"

"They arrested Andy Bragg—"

"—and let him go—"

"—and Johnson will haul him in again," Paul said. "If you keep your nose out of it and don't do something crazy!"

"Johnson, the guy who blew George Kurtz's case? Well, *that's* a relief!"

The silence was deafening.

Finally Paul spoke. "Johnson's sharper than he looks. He cut Bragg loose because one of Bragg's clients is a high-powered lawyer. But they'll rearrest him and make it stick."

Ice clinked again, and Lily thought of the theater's alcove. The stifling heat. Vanessa in that felt cloche and heavy coat, blood dripping from her throat to the fur collar and down her sleeve. Did the killer make her put on the coat and gloves? Lily struggled with her own gloves sometimes; how hard would it be to force leather over lifeless fingers? "Who else are they looking at, Paul?"

"Besides Bragg? You know I can't—"

"Check out Laird Bennett."

"Who?" But Paul didn't sound curious, or surprised. "Why don't you think it's Bragg?"

"Because Vanessa's murderer made her dress up before he cut her throat. Does that sound like a testosterone-crazed bodybuilder?"

Paul's chair screeched. This was a shitty thing to throw at him on the eve of a Senate hearing, but she needed his help. "Look into Bennett," she pleaded. "He left the Kennedy Center."

Now Paul was pacing. "And you wonder why I'm begging you to move to D.C.?"

She gripped the phone. "You saw the crime scene photos, Paul." She waited for him to deny it. "What about her shoes?"

"Aha!" he exclaimed. "Not the director—the costumer!"

"The killer knows Hopper, Paul." It sounded crazy out loud.

"Must be pretty old. Hopper died sixty years ago."

"But the props, the details—"

"Oh, I get it! You had dinner with your old man."

And there it was, as livid and accusatory as his scar. Saving Dad from Kurtz's killer had almost cost Paul his life. He blamed Dad, but the choice to run out on Paul had been hers. If she could go back to that filthy shack, would she run out on him again?

"Details please, Lily," Paul continued, "weigh them like a sack of mail. Only trust what you yourself can see, right?" For a guy who'd met Dad for two seconds, Paul had him down. "His game's rigged, Lily."

"Sounds like you're the one who's sick of playing."

"Maybe I am."

She cast about desperately to fill the silence.

"Look into Bennett," she begged.

"Why not?" His weary laugh cut to the bone. "If you consider moving to D.C."

"Paul—"

"Deal or not?"

"Deal."

Chapter Seven

In a silver bob and satin-collared tux, the petite woman took The Kurtz Auditorium stage. Against its scarlet backdrop, she brought Denver a touch of Weimar cabaret.

Gina led the applause.

"Let's welcome Sasha Lazar, esteemed scholar, cherished colleague, and world expert on Edward Hopper!" Gina moved in for an embrace. Sasha stepped back, converting Gina's peck to an air kiss. The two women had never actually met, but Sasha had edited Gina's essay for the Hopper catalog so many times the print still bled. Sasha set her iPad on the lectern and waited for Gina to take her seat with Michel in the front row.

At the rear of the auditorium there was a commotion. Lily turned to look. Laird Bennett had just arrived with the kid in black from the theater. The only empty seat was in the middle of a row. Waving to the audience like he was directing the show, Bennett climbed over patrons to reach it. When the ruckus subsided, Sasha began.

"My dear friend Michel asked me to talk about Hopper's influence on film noir." Michel wagged his finger back at her playfully. "His clapboard houses, gas stations, and urban skylines, his clerks working late and last customers at the bar. Wikipedia claims they reek of alienation and cigarette smoke." She shrugged. "But let's depart from the script."

Michel stiffened.

"And I thought I'd be bored," Elena cackled.

"Not on Angela's dime," Lily whispered back.

Sasha signaled the AV booth. The screen behind her lit.

"*Summer Interior*, 1909," Sasha said. A disheveled young woman in a skimpy chemise slumped on the floor by an unmade bed. Footboard, mantel, and window seemed to pin her there. Her hand rested limply between her naked legs. Lily did the math; Hopper painted it three years after *Couple with Poplars*. Was she the prim Gibson Girl with upswept hair and smart leather boots?

"Lordy!" Elena whispered. "What happened to him in Paris?"

Click.

"*Summer Evening*, 1947." A blonde girl and her date leaned against the rail of a wooden porch. It was evening, and they were dressed like they'd come from the beach or a park. In chinos and a dark T-shirt, he leaned toward the girl imploringly, while she, in pink bandeau and shorts, stared sullenly down. Sasha sighed. "Will that poor boy ever get his kiss?"

Click.

"*Room in New York*, 1940." An apartment window opened onto a couple in evening dress. The woman sat at an upright piano, her hand absently touching a key, and the man was absorbed in a newspaper. Separated by a small table, they were continents apart.

More clicks. Diners, hotel rooms. With a suitcase or valise as props, a stony blonde with pointy breasts stood or sat, depicted in profile or looking down. The clicks came faster and she became a blur. "You may notice Hopper kept painting the same woman," Sasha said. "His wife, Jo Nivison, was a talented artist who lost her identity when she married him. She got even by insisting on being his only model…"

Chuckles from the audience.

"… that way she never aged."

A keynote's fun was the promise of delicious gossip about the artist's private life. Warming to their enthusiasm, Sasha clicked to an early 1900s photograph of a lively girl in a high-necked blouse and sporty military-style cap. "This is Enid Marie Saies. While she studied at the Sorbonne, she roomed at Hopper's boarding house. They went to the Opera and Versailles. He made her laugh…"

Patrons leaned forward in their seats.

"…Intent on marriage, he followed Enid back to England and sat in her garden while she embroidered a waistcoat. She asked him to help her by biting off threads…"

Michel whispered urgently to Gina. She waved at Sasha.

Sasha ignored them. "Unfortunately, the waistcoat was for a dashing Frenchman to whom Enid was already engaged!" The audience gasped and groaned. "Realizing how degrading this was, Hopper recoiled and vowed he wouldn't do that for another man. He wired his mother for money and never crossed the Atlantic again." Sasha paused to let that sink in, then continued brightly. "And then there was Alta Hilsdale, a Minnesota socialite whose parents sent her to Paris so she could become a suitable wife. Hopper painted her…"

Click.

Deep-set eyes stared inexpressively from the portrait, so shadowed and impenetrable the skin around them looked bruised. A spread-collar blouse revealed a pallid expanse of skin. The only note of color was her lips, reddish and full. She was as sullen as the girl in the pink bandeau and as carnal and despondent as the one in the chemise on the bedroom floor.

"What happened?" someone called out.

"Funny you should ask," Sasha said. "A trove of letters from Enid was recently discovered in Hopper's boyhood attic. Dozens and dozens of excuses—"

Michel leapt to his feet. "*Merci mille fois* to our distinguished—"

"Dear me!" Sasha glanced at her watch and grinned. "The wine and cheese."

Click.

"*Cape Cod Evening*, 1939." A defeated man in work pants and a white T-shirt slumped on the stoop of a framed house. The blonde in the doorway behind him glared as he tried to get the attention of a collie in the foreground who gamboled in tall grass. Sasha sighed. "Domestic bliss."

Laughs.

Sasha's pointer lingered on the dog. Tail high, body stiff, alert to a sound only it could hear. Unleashed, the dog was the only subject in the painting that was truly alive. Gina stood and began to clap. Like the collie, Sasha ignored her again. "Questions?" She scanned the audience and stopped at the kid in black from the theater.

"What's with the dog?" he asked.

"Bravo!" Sasha said. "Hopper broke his own rule. Why not paint kids or pets?"

He smiled impishly. "Because they won't sit still. Seriously, how'd he get that dog to pose?"

"There were no collies in Truro, so he went to the library for a picture. As usual, his wife Jo came to the rescue. She spotted one in a car and played with it long enough for him to sketch it."

Laird Bennett waved. "Who's the gal in *Summer Interior*?" The disheveled one by the unmade bed.

"Good question—"

Michel leapt to the stage. "*Merci infiniment!*" he cried. "And now for refreshments."

—

Lily got Elena some crackers and pâté. Across the room, James was handing the Objects Conservator's beguiling assistant a tonic with lime—a smooth move for an art handler. Matt watched them despondently.

"Gonna let him get away with that?" Lily asked.

"I don't know what—"

"What's her name?"

"Willow."

"Fetch Willow some cheese, Matt. And a real drink."

"But she—"

"Make her laugh!" Lily pushed him toward a waiter and watched him grab two glasses of Chardonnay.

Angela came over and gave Lily and Elena an affectionate hug. "Sasha's honorarium was worth every cent!" she gloated.

"You told her to toss the script?" Lily asked.

"We go way back." Angela got a refill from the waiter and slipped a twenty in his belt. "You didn't know I went to Yale? Sasha is Hopper's dog—she won't be leashed." She tossed down her wine. "But I did promise her more than cheap wine. Join us?"

"Bedtime for me, alas," Elena said. She turned to Lily. "You go, dear. I'll hail a Lyft."

Across the room, Matt was making Willow laugh. Angela could drink a truckdriver under the table, and tomorrow was a workday. "I'll pass," Lily said.

Angela's face fell. "We're still on for tomorrow's flash mob, right?"

"Of course." Michel's gamble on not canceling the gala had paid off. *The Post* and the alt weekly had run features about Hopper over the weekend, and ticket sales for the exhibition were booming. Gina's assistant had already tweeted out the second micro-drama's location: Civic Center Park at noon. Through the crowd, Sasha was waving at Angela with a get-me-outta-here look. "I'll drive you, Elena," Lily said. "Give me a sec." She fetched two fresh glasses of wine and went over to Sasha.

"Lily, right?" Sasha accepted the wine and took a healthy sip. "Angela filled me in on the murder. How meta."

"Meta?" Lily said.

"Pardon my Yale. Death commenting on art."

"So you don't think it was the boyfriend?"

"The way she was posed?" Sasha snorted. "Hopper's obviously the draw, or his woman. And having gotten away with it, why stop?" Across the floor, Gina brandished a bottle of gin but was waylaid by Laird Bennett. Lily led Sasha to a quieter corner.

"Angela also told me about you." Sasha's eyes were shrewd. "Describe the scene."

Lily told her about the mirror, coat, gloves, snack plate—the fuck-me's. "They're not in *Automat*, but Vanessa did wear them onstage…."

Sasha leaned in. "But?"

Lily pictured the straps cutting into Vanessa's ankles. "They were the wrong size…."

Sasha nodded, and her silver bob glinted under the overhead light.

"…and the wrong color! Onstage they were silver; the ones Vanessa was killed in were blue. He made her wear a different pair."

"He wasn't worried he'd be caught." Sasha glanced around. "Why, he may even—"

"Sasha!" Gina snatched the professor's wineglass and thrust a tumbler of gin into her hand. "If we can kidnap you, Michel—"

"Oh, dear." Sasha set down the gin. "Angela's taking me to the airport. The Kurtz Foundation's personal touch."

Gina tried to hide her disappointment. "Next time."

Sasha turned to Lily and gestured. *Call me.*

Chapter Eight

There she is across the floor, hobnobbing and sipping wine. What's she thinking? You feel a stir, let it build. You like not knowing, it's okay—for now. Because maybe she's The One.

You smile at the girl minding the table with the cheese. That unisex black waitstaff garb doesn't do a thing for her. Hands folded stiffly behind her back, like she's stolen the cheap silverware, she looks past your shoulder. You don't bother looking behind you. There's nobody exciting at this reception, she just doesn't want to look at you. You're used to being invisible. But not to The One, who took her time looking in the alcove at Offbeat on Thursday night.

You had no way of knowing it would be her, of course—a gift of fate. From across the theater's lobby you watched her knock, then go in. And waited an eternity for the denouement. Where was the commotion, where was the scream? Instead of immediately backing out, she closed the door behind her. And spent quite a bit of time inside. Minutes ticked, the party in the lobby played on. Finally she emerged, a trifle pale, clutching her purse. She quietly closed the door behind her and stood in front of it composing herself. After an eternity she pulled out her phone and calmly summoned help. It was better than a scream.

You watch her now, working the crowd. She's with the preening professor from Yale who thinks she knows Hopper. Enough to recognize what you did in the alcove? You laugh to yourself. Yale got everything about Hopper and the boy and girl on *Summer Evening*'s porch all wrong. But she'll get hers, because details matter. Because you yourself have been on that very same porch, with The Girl.

A waiter with a tray of red wine scurries past. You grab one and spill it on his neat stack of cocktail napkins. He shakes his head in disgust and rushes off. You set your wine on a table with the other trash. At evening's end, it'll end up where the girl at the cheese table and all the ones like her belong. The Girl may be eternal, but she is not immortal. You may have to prove that again.

High school was where you first met The Girl. She was soft, kind, attentive, pink. The first girl who really listened. She thought you were smart. She shared your passions, laughed at your jokes. She had daddy issues. You let down your guard and told her about mom. You bought The Girl bath salts and perfume. You couldn't afford them, she could; they all thought she was out of your league, but she accepted your gifts with her tinselly laugh because they came from you. No touching for now—that could wait. Just the laugh. For the first time, you weren't the loser they all thought.

You stole a locket from a jewelry store at the mall, a gold chain with a 14-karat scalloped heart. You wrapped it in tissue and tied it in a box with pink ribbon. She opened it and her eyes went wide. You kissed her hard on the mouth. She reared back and wiped her lips. Her eyes narrowed. That Look was a stun-gun bolt to your heart.

Next day, everyone pointed and laughed. Her laugh was no longer music; now it was a jeer. You skipped classes and steered clear of the cafeteria. You dropped out of drama club. The school sent home notes. You transferred and barely graduated. Did she plan it all along, how many boys had she done it to? *You'll be fine*, mom said, *there will be other girls*. But it took years to make sense of the wreckage she made of your life, the smoking crater she left for your heart. That bitch walked away without a scratch, and you moved on.

Then, one day in an art survey course, you came across *Summer Evening*. The boy in chinos and deck shoes, The Girl's sullen superiority and scorn. Your head rang with jeers, it was like being kicked in the nuts all over again! How could Hopper know how it felt to want and plead, to look but not touch?

You devoured everything about him and his work and his women. That's how you met Alta. Her letters—you read them all. *I should enjoy it very much to go to Saint Cloud, but I really don't see when I could do it... I think I shall have to put off the Café d'Harcourt for this week.* How she busted his balls! *I am sorry I shall not be in Saturday evening—will you come Tuesday instead?* Even a hundred years ago, a guy knew what Tuesday meant! *Certainly I might have spared you one evening this week—I might also have spared several other people one evening—and where would my evenings have been?*

Now Hopper's come to town.

"May I have some brie, miss?" you ask the girl at the cheese table. She's confused—others are helping themselves. You want her to give you a little napkin and plate, force her to unclasp her soft pink hands. "Never mind," you say with a wink. You take a tissue from your pocket and wipe your lips, then crumple it and drop it by the platter of cheese. Her hands rise to her mouth. Then she snatches the tissue with her fingertips and drops it on the floor behind the table.

You look again at Lily. She's helping an old bat—the gallerist—into her ridiculous opera cape. They'll leave and you'll be left. At the cheese table, the girl has summoned another member of the catering staff. She whispers urgently and points, and you give them a friendly wave. You could wait until after... No, let her ponder her mistake. You've made a few yourself—*should've wrapped that fucking 14-carat gold locket around The Girl's throat!*—but tonight won't be one. Will Lily accept your gifts?

It's time for fun.

Chapter Nine

In bed, Lily opened her laptop. If the world's expert on Edward Hopper believed the killer was drawn to the artist and wouldn't stop, she'd better find a place to start. Skipping over his paintings on the web, she began searching for clues in Hopper's past.

Click. Hopper grew up in Nyack, New York. By age eleven, he was over six feet tall. Shy, introverted, bullied at school—no wonder. Click. His mild-mannered father had a failed dry-goods store, and his mother, Elizabeth Griffiths Smith, was a strict Baptist who wielded the purse.

Click. An oil portrait of Elizabeth. Deep lines accentuated unsmiling lips. Sunken eyes staring unflinchingly at the artist from under untamed brows that arched as if to say, *whom do you think you're fooling, boy?* Maybe Hopper had caught her on a bad day, but except for the silky white knot of hair and her purple taffeta dress, Elizabeth Griffiths Smith could have been a man. Click. In Hopper's middle-aged self-portrait, his mother's grim features were transposed onto his smooth bald head.

Click. A 1908 photograph of Hopper in Paris. The young artist was a stork in stiff tweeds, a kid dressing up as a banker. Gazing pensively into the distance in his straw boater and with a sketchpad at his knee, he pursed his heavy lips. Did something happen to him there?

Click. His first letter home to Elizabeth, 1906, rang with scorn:

> *The Frenchmen for the most part are small and have poor physiques. You will not see here as you do on "Broadway" the finely built young fellows with their strong, well cut features. However, the French must conceal "the goods" somehow or other, as we know they are on the spot when the time comes, in spite of their little beards & long shoes…*

Was Hopper referring to their military prowess, or their reputation in the sack? Unless he was trying to get a rise out of his straight-laced Baptist mother, it seemed a strange thing to confide in her. But according to Sasha, he'd struck out with the girls—

Ping. Paul? Lily grabbed her phone.

A text from Sasha. *Speaking of Hopper's women…*

A scanned letter was attached. Postmarked 1908, it was from Alta Hilsdale in Minnesota, to Hopper in Nyack. In flowing cursive, Alta gushed about wanting to spend time in New York before returning to Paris. Lily yawned. Paul would never let her hear the end of going down a hundred-year-old rabbit hole. No matter what Sasha believed, a killer identifying with an artist who'd felt physically inadequate but done nothing more offensive than wield a paintbrush was starting to feel pretty silly. And it was getting late. She began to close the file, then noticed Alta's letter went onto a second page.

> *Do you know, I had a very alarming dream about you awhile ago— you tried to throw me down a cliff or something, and I had an awful time trying to save my life—I decided you must be hating me very hard to cause such a dream and I wondered if it is because I have never answered your note asking when I was going to be in New York again…*

What the hell—did Alta really think the man who wanted to have sex with her was capable of throwing her off a cliff?

Lily read it again.

This went beyond the indignity of biting off threads only to learn the waistcoat belonged to a love object's fiancé. Or enduring the humiliation of dozens of excuses for why a woman didn't want to see you. It wasn't just that Alta feared she'd pushed him too far. She actually thought he hated her enough to be capable of killing her.

Ping. Another text from Sasha.

Girlie Show 1941.

Lily scrolled to it on her phone.

The woman in Hopper's painting was cold and hard, but not enigmatic. She had black-rimmed eyes and ruby lips, and her chin jutted like her scarlet-tipped missile-shaped breasts. With a diaphanous blue drape billowing behind her, she pranced across an elevated stage in closed-toe blue fuck-me's with ankle straps.

Chapter Ten

Angela Kurtz sank onto the bench at Civic Center Park.

"Where's the flash mob?" she demanded. "And whose idea was this anyway?"

"Gina's," Lily replied.

Angela took off her strappy sandal and massaged her foot. "Remind me to fire her."

"You could've cancelled Hopper."

"When Michel compared me to George, I almost did. They know damn well what a prick my father was! With his exes and mistresses—"

Including Gina.

"At least he had the good sense to leave everything to you," Lily reminded her.

It was noon and food trucks lined the hot pavement. Latin-Asian fusion, vegan, ribs. Office workers jousted for tables with umbrellas, a busker swallowed his sword, street musicians strummed, and pot hung in the air. Angela fanned away the fumes. "Remind me to send Gina my dry-cleaning bill." On the opposite bench a sad-faced mime wiped a tear. She limped over and dropped a fiver in his hat. "At least he keeps his mouth shut."

"Hungover, are we?" Lily said.

Angela groaned. "Sasha has a wooden leg. Did you two solve the murder?"

"She referred me to Hopper's woman." Lily told her about *Girlie Show*.

"To a feminist, it's always the dame," Angela said. "Seriously, Lily, tell me you're not getting involved. George's murder was one thing, but…"

"Too late for that. I found Vanessa, remember?"

Angela squinted at her. "And with the DPD so out to lunch, how lucky you did. Which reminds me I'm starving. How about L'Atelier?"

"But what if Sasha's right and the killer shows up?" Lily said.

"If he's dumb enough to attack at noon in Civic Center Park, even the DPD can catch him."

Drawn like lemmings by the food trucks, office workers streamed into the park. If a flash mob actually formed, Lily had to admit Gina's micro-dramas—actors posing mutely like Hoppers and then springing to life—were marketing genius. She scanned for a break in the action that might signal something about to occur. Amid the Brownian motion at the north colonnade, two figures stood stock still. She grabbed Angela's hand. "I found it!"

They hurried over.

Against a sandstone column framed by traffic and the churning crowd, a young couple posed. The blonde wore pink shorts flared high on the thigh and a matching bandeau. Her breasts thrust forward provocatively, but she gazed sullenly at the pastel flats on her feet. The boy wore chinos and a T-shirt. He leaned in with his hand imploringly raised. In *Summer Evening*'s postwar version of *Couple's* Gibson Girl and Beret Man, the blonde ignored him.

Angela pumped her fist. "You go, sister!"

A horn blasted but the actors held their poses.

From behind the column, the kid in black from the theater emerged. With birdlike motions, he adjusted the actress's bandeau and lowered the actor's elbow an inch. The gestures were tiny but they brought Hopper's painting into focus. It was a hot summer night. The colonnade was a white porch, and the couple leaned on the wood railing.

Stepping back, the kid in black almost bumped into Lily. He smiled apologetically, revealing an appealing gap in his front teeth as he introduced himself.

"Ernie Dale, Offbeat's stage manager." He scarcely looked old enough to vote, let alone run a theater's lighting and sets.

"You were at the lecture last night," Lily said.

"And you're the lady who found Vanessa." Ernie knelt to point the actress's flats ever so slightly away from the actor's deck shoes. He tugged her shorts down to make them a touch more discreet, and she gave a tiny grateful nod. "Rachel and Bo are real troupers."

Gina's tweets must not be getting out; office workers and hard hats detoured around them without the slightest show of interest. Bo suppressed a sneeze. "Allergies," Ernie explained. Even aside from their fellow actor being murdered, it felt weird to talk about them as if they weren't there. It reminded Lily of an experimental play she'd gone to with Elena. They'd been the only ones in the audience and had spread out to make the theater feel full. How much worse it must have been for the actors! Ernie gently lowered Bo's chin a notch.

"Just right," Angela said.

Ernie shrugged. "Art's in the details."

"So you're an artist?" Angela said.

A blush crept up his neck. "If you count painting scenery and staging sets."

Lily jumped in. "I bet you hate actors banging into walls and knocking over props!"

"At least the paintings you work on hold still." Ernie sighed heavily. "The show goes on, but this is hell." Finally drawn by the little troupe, two ladies with foil-wrapped burritos had stopped. A techie joined them. "Ready, kids?" Ernie murmured. Rachel popped something into her mouth, and Bo drew a breath.

Stepping to the center of the colonnade, Ernie loudly cleared his throat. More passers-by paused. He stepped smartly to the center of the colonnade with a wooden clapperboard. *The Denver Art Museum* was written on the slate.

"Edward Hopper, Take Two." Ernie raised the board and slammed the clapper. "Action!"

Rachel stepped forward. Hands on hips, she turned to Bo with her eyebrows theatrically raised. Freed from her Hopperian sulk, she was quite pretty.

"Oh my God, as if I'd go to the prom with you!" Rachel popped her chewing gum loudly. "Like, I saw you with Karen. You're totally asking me because she turned you down." The techie in the audience laughed. Encouraged, Rachel wriggled her shoulders. "Like, did you ask Marla and Debbie too?"

Bo raised his hands defensively and stepped back. "But—"

"No way! Like, just look at your bogus deck shoes."

A construction worker hooted.

Bo looked down in consternation. "I thought you liked these shoes."

Rachel rolled her eyes. "As if!"

More people were stopping. They took out smartphones and began filming. Bo turned to the audience and winked.

"And like, why would I want to go to dinner with you?" Rachel continued. She cracked her gum again. "You don't know how to act on a date. Like that time at McDonald's. You ate French fries with your mouth open, it totally had to be the-worst-date-*ever*!"

"I wonder if Edward Hopper ate French fries," Bo mused to the crowd. "You think one of our greatest American painters had this much trouble getting a date?"

Rachel pursed her lips. "But I said no to Tom and Biff, and I *really* want to go to the prom…" She turned to the audience. "Would you, like, go with him?"

"He'd have to buy me a helluva dinner!" Angela called out.

"And a corsage!" another woman cried.

"Totally." Rachel nodded and turned back to Bo. "And a limo. And wear that awesome dinner jacket of yours."

Bo scratched his head. "Would you go with her?" he asked the audience.

"Hell, yeah!" a hard hat cried.

"But do we have to go through this every time?" Bo said.

The crowd roared.

Rachel grabbed Bo and gave him a lusty kiss. The audience cheered and the actors did a happy, sloppy bow. Rachel hugged Bo, then waved to the crowd. "And after the prom, we'll see you a week from Saturday at The Denver Art Museum's Edward Hopper show!"

The audience applauded again and began putting away their smartphones.

"Great job," Ernie told Bo and Rachel. "Take twenty."

Bo grabbed Rachel's hand and they ran off to the food trucks.

"Terrific!" Lily said. "Rachel's a natural, and Bo's a helluva straight man."

"The riff's a tad retro," Angela said grudgingly, "but they knocked it out of the park. Did Cam Maddox script it?"

"Rach did some improv," Ernie said.

He didn't seem to think much of the mustachioed playwright, but onlookers were still laughing, and it wasn't just the actors. Cam had taken *Summer Evening's* flustered boy and sullen girl in a totally unexpected direction. Lily looked around. If the killer was fixated on Hopper, could he resist staying away? And if he'd come, what did he make of Cam's riff?

"When's the next show?" Lily asked.

Ernie shuffled his feet. "Thursday."

Two days. "Which Hopper will it be?" she asked.

"If I told you, Gina would kill me." He saw her expression. "Sorry, not funny."

"C'mon, Ernie," Angela wheedled, "is it another Valley Girl riff?"

"Ask Kip."

The museum's mount-maker was coordinating with the theater. But

Vanessa had been murdered at Offbeat, and the killer liked props.

"Know what?" Lily said. "I've never been backstage. But that must be Cam's domain."

Ernie looked at her shrewdly. "Meet me in the lobby at six."

Chapter Eleven

You watch *Summer Evening* in the park.

Hopper would love it!

Valley Girl is a wind-up doll. A hard hat roars as he waits for her to run down. And oh, boy, when she does... Yale's lit-crit shit last night still rankles. *Does the poor boy get his kiss?* Well, guess what, Yale—Valley Girl's talking herself into what he wanted all along! This is more like it. The Boy's looking good, he's got the crowd on his side. He doesn't have to teach her a lesson. He doesn't have to do a damn thing.

The actors kiss like they mean business.

The construction worker pumps his fist, secretaries hoist their burritos in a salute.

Hail to The Boy! Two to nothing, counting Vanessa. Guess what, Yale? This is how *Summer Evening* is meant to end. And it's so very personal, because that painting is an icon. It brought you to art class and the Model. Again the hand of fate, but this one schooled you well. You'll never forget that first day.

Figure drawing is essential, the teacher had said, the foundation of art. Photos were no substitute, not even the ones on the web. At easels in a semicircle around a platform with an empty stool, you and the others flipped open your sketchbooks and raised your pencils. The Model padded in barefoot, in a kimono that had seen better days. Looking at no one, she dropped her kimono and arranged herself on the stool.

The Model was blonde like The Girl, but older. Her features were hard, her face had no expression. She did not speak. No talking to her or touching was allowed. Only Teacher could address her. Like a theater's fourth wall, there was an illusion to protect. She posed standing, sitting and lying down; your favorite was her slouching on the stool. She did it three hours on end. For five-minute breaks, she donned her kimono and left the studio floor. At the end of class, you were always the last to leave.

One night you waited in the parking lot. I have something for you, you said. You gave her the box with the ribbon. Her eyes narrowed and she shook her head. You opened it and showed her the pink satin robe. She pushed it away and gave you that look.

Blood rushed to your head. Your fists clenched. She backed off and quickly drove away. You dropped the robe and stood there watching her taillights disappear and holding the sash. *I could have used this on her…* Like Alta, she shouldn't have gotten away with it. Next day before class, Teacher took you aside. Don't come back, he said. You packed up your pencils and sketchbook. It wasn't her ratting you out. It was The Look.

That night you searched the web. Not for a woman, but for men like you, guys you could mentor. Men who knew what it meant to be treated like trash, to look at a woman and have pity and contempt stare back. Because *Summer Evening* proved you weren't alone, and even stupid twits like Alta and Valley Girl knew when they'd pushed a man too far. You'd give them what they were begging for, pick up where Hopper himself left off. And you wouldn't get caught.

Lunch is over in the park. Buskers and the homeless reign again, and *Summer Evening* is rewritten. The Boy ends up on top.

But that kiss.

Did Valley Girl have to enjoy it quite so much?

Chapter Twelve

"Hello?" Lily called.

Offbeat's lobby was empty, and the box office was dark. The door to the alcove had crime scene tape, but the red velour curtain to the auditorium still carried a hint of patchouli. Days ago, it had welcomed her to an enchanted world; now it was pulled shut, and Offbeat had the air of a host who hadn't wanted guests in the first place.

The curtain parted. Ernie's round head hung between its folds like a moon, and the air around him seemed to dance. His black attire hid all but his face.

"You should be an actor!" Lily said.

"It's more fun pulling the ropes."

"Isn't that Laird's job?" she asked.

His smile faded. "Takes more than him and Cam to run a circus." He held the curtain for her, and she followed him into the auditorium.

Seats tilted forward like playgoers before a curtain's rise. The stage itself seemed inhabited by ghosts; the pedestal table with saucer and cup awaited Vanessa. But if the lobby and auditorium were a graveyard, backstage was a medieval village. In dark clothing and sturdy boots, the crew bustled about a warren of dressing rooms, storage areas, and workshops like craftsmen in a fellowship of guilds.

"You make the scenery and props?" Lily asked.

"We're pretty resourceful; what we can't do in-house, we rent or scrounge." Apparently there was nothing sacred about the props, but Ernie was too modest about his achievements: Offbeat had won awards for his *Sweeney Todd* and *Rope* sets. A burly fellow stopped to confer with him about a backdrop. Then a guy with tats had a question about a curtain's slider.

"Physics," Ernie told them.

He poked his head in the carpentry shop. "Tie back your hair, Randy!" The guy at the lathe made a peace sign and wound his hair into a manbun. "And put on your damn goggles!"

A frowning woman with an armload of costumes strode down the corridor, followed by a man with a coil of wire. Ernie stood back to let them pass. "The new production is Rachel's breakout," he explained. "This time it's a real script, not one of Cam's riffs."

At a section partitioned by dividers, Ernie knocked at a door. Rachel answered in a robe. "We're not interrupting?" he asked.

"No, no," she said. "Come in."

The tiny dressing room held a vanity and chair. Bo stood in the corner. Hair gel and a tight silk shirt had remade Hopper's pleading boy into a fashion-forward metrosexual.

"Whew," Ernie said. "Hours in the sun, then a rehearsal."

"We're fine," Rachel insisted. On the vanity lay a vest with fancy stitching.

Ernie frowned. "Still sewing for Maria? I'll talk to Laird—"

"No!" Rachel laughed to soften it. "It relaxes me, and I'm almost done." She gave Bo the vest. It fit perfectly, but a thread from the stitchery hung loose. She searched in vain for scissors, then held the garment out to Ernie. "You mind?"

Blushing, he bit off the thread.

"Not a word to Maria," Rachel warned. She dabbed her cheeks with coconut oil and began toweling off her foundation. It seemed stubborn as varnish.

"Gently," Ernie said, "and easy on the mascara."

"Yes, boss." She rolled her eyes at Lily.

"Ernie?" A welder was at the door. "We need you."

"C'mon, Bo," Ernie said. With a long glance at Rachel, Bo left too.

Next to the mirror was a publicity shot of Vanessa in a low-cut Victorian dress and heavy eye makeup. "Vee was Mrs. Lovett," Rachel said, referring to Sweeney Todd's lover who turned his victims into mince pies. Vanessa's fleshy shoulders and coarse makeup reminded Lily the actress had been older than she'd appeared onstage. Rachel seemed to read her mind. "Vee got *Automat* because she could vamp. She and Andy worked hard to drop the weight she put on for *Sweeney*. But a woman's hands never lie."

"You were great today," Lily said. "What'd you think of the script?"

Rachel focused on the mirror. "It was fun—not sexist, if that's what you mean. Vee looked forward to it, too. I was lucky to be her understudy."

"And now you're stepping in."

Rachel glanced up sharply. "There's always more actresses than roles. You never expect to become friends. Vee was both."

"Tell me about Andy Bragg," Lily said.

"He's not as dumb as he looks," Rachel said. "Neither is Bo."

"But Vanessa filed an assault charge…"

"That was bullshit." Rachel reached for the eyeliner and drew a strong line under her lower lash. "Laird caught them."

"Who?"

"Andy and Vee. It was late, she thought they were alone." Rachel looked at the photo again and tried to soften the line. "Laird creeps around at night. Luckily Ernie stepped in and saved her job. Laird thinks he owns us."

Lily crossed Andy off the suspect list. "What about Cam?"

"He brings us gifts."

"Gifts?"

"Chocolates, lipstick. A latte or a snack."

Cam Maddox jumped to the top of the list.

Chapter Thirteen

Artemesia Gentileschi's gentlelady stared up at Lily from the conservation lab's vacuum-heat table. With the last of the Hoppers now in the exhibition gallery, the 1640 portrait had resumed center stage. As Lily leaned in to examine damage to the portrait, she felt an odd kinship with its subject. She rubbed her forearm absently.

"Your skin graft?" Matt asked sympathetically.

"It itches," Lily admitted.

Like it always did when she stood at the massive suction table on which George Kurtz's killer had thrown her after heating it to 160 degrees. He'd done worse to Paul, but the graft made her self-conscious and for the past year she'd been wearing long sleeves. Her colleagues never asked about her change in style; who wanted to think about working at such a dangerous piece of equipment, much less being attacked in their sanctum sanctorum? As for killers, if Vanessa's was at the park, he'd done nothing to make his presence known, and even Angela thought she should lay off. Lily refocused on the gash in the portrait's cheek.

"At least there's no fungus," Matt pointed out.

"All she needs is athlete's foot," Lily agreed.

"Too bad you can't give her a real makeover," James said. The handler was hanging around the lab a lot. He and Matt were hitting it off—or was it because the beguiling Willow was cleaning a bust of Artemis in the adjoining room? But Matt and James were right.

Even before the neglect, abuse and assaults, Gentileschi's lady wasn't pretty. Her hair was coarse and unruly, she had a cleft chin, and her eyes bulged. They'd cleaned and relined her and scraped an inept previous restorer's jarring gray pigment down to white patches resembling impetigo. Because viewers expected her to age gracefully, they'd left the craquelure. But now it was time for cosmetic integration, and like a facelift, the question was always how much.

"We can in-paint to recompose her face…" Matt began.

"… or make the restoration visually distinct," James said, "so the viewer isn't deceived."

Lily nodded. "Bravo, James!"

"If Gina lets you."

"Gina?" she said.

"I've been around the art world," he said good-naturedly. "Believe me, I've met worse."

He glanced at Willow, who was tenderly patting an agar poultice onto the bust. Matt had better move fast; James didn't need to be told to fetch her a drink at Sasha's reception, and despite his mild demeanor and hint of a paunch, he was sharp enough to get the distinction between art and artifice. Not that Matt wasn't, but he was so gob-smacked by Willow that these days she needed a semaphore to communicate with him.

Lily turned back to James. "How'd you become a handler?"

"Packed and shipped for a gallery in college," he said, "then bought a van. I ran into Kip doing jobs for the museum. A guy on his crew quit, and he hired me full-time for Hopper."

If he worked with Kip, he'd know where the next flash mob would be. Obviously he had no affection for Gina; if she got him to tip her off, she and Angela could go early and scope out the crowd. "James, do you suppose—"

He gave her a subtle nod.

"Lily!" Gina had slunk in behind them. "How nice to see you actually work." She directed a fishy look at James. "Why aren't you helping Kip?"

"I swung by to grab Matt for lunch. Mad Greens, remember?" He nudged Matt, who gave a guilty start. "Can we bring something back?" he asked Lily.

"No thanks." They left, and Lily turned to Gina. "What's up?"

"Ticket sales are spiking."

"Michel must be thrilled." She waited for the next shoe to drop.

"Have you talked to Sasha lately?" Gina held out her phone. "I've been getting these crazy cartoons."

Lily scrolled through them. More like caricatures than cartoons, the drawings were in a 1930s style. A curly-haired woman perched saucily on a cloud, reading a book and ignoring the skeleton below her begging for food. In the next she sat upright in bed, swathed like a nun in a high-necked dressing gown and veil, and gesturing imperiously at the emaciated fellow in apron and halo who bowed deeply to her from the floor. The last was a cluster of disembodied floating objects: a curly topknot, earrings, collar, cuffs and heels. The woman herself had been erased.

"Are these by Hopper?" Lily asked.

"No idea." Gina shrugged, but she was understandably upset. The caricatures were funny but not. "Someone's being clever. Just wondered if you were in the loop."

Trust her to turn it into a personal coup. "How long have you been getting them?"

"Since Sasha's lecture," Gina said.

"Can I send them to her?"

"Don't you dare!" Gina snatched back her phone. "It's probably a fan."

Of hers—or Hopper's? "Was there a note?"

"No. Stop grilling me, Lily!"

"What name did he use?"

Gina sighed. "He calls himself Hoppin' Mad. Untraceable, of course." She rolled her eyes, but she'd been worried enough to run it by a geek on her staff. "Maybe my admirer will announce himself at the gala."

Or sooner. "Where's the next flash mob?"

Gina wagged her finger. "You'll find out soon enough."

———

In bed, Lily searched for Jo Nivison on her laptop. A photograph of Hopper in dour middle-age showed him with a petite busty woman with curly hair and a pointy chin who stared defiantly into the camera. His wife Jo—the woman in the caricatures.

The phone beeped.

"Bennett left the Kennedy Center under a cloud," Paul said.

"Cumulonimbus?" Her joke fell flat.

"Let Johnson handle it." That was becoming a familiar refrain, but Paul sounded genuinely beat.

"Something soured you on Andy Bragg?"

"Nothing's changed, Lily. I don't give a rat's ass—"

"Whoa! You called me."

"—about this case, and neither should you." He took a breath. "Look, Lily, I know what your job means to you. And Hopper. Don't risk all you've worked for, for an actress you never met."

"Doesn't finding her dead count?" she said.

"Not funny."

Paul was right, and about more than that. Angela's rep was on the line, and Elena's gallery was on the ropes. Keep digging and she might not be the only one who paid. "After Mark's confirmed—"

"Tomorrow changes nothing, Lily. I thought Hopper would."

They'd talked about it—daydreamed, really. The show's success would spring her from under Michel's and Gina's thumb. She and Angela would fly around the country assembling blockbusters, and as a private conservator, she could in-paint a Gentileschi without being deceptive. But someone was calling himself Hoppin' Mad, and what if Sasha was right?

"So Bennett left D.C. under a cloud," she said.

The silence stretched.

Finally Paul spoke. "The Phillips is looking for a conservator."

"Oh?"

"I found a condo on Dupont Circle."

"Little fast, isn't it? What about your lease?"

"It's month-to-month."

"I thought we'd look together."

"If I waited for that—"

—you—

"—I'd be too old to care."

Not enough for a man like him or a woman like her. Before his brush with death, they'd wasted ten years apart. Elena called their arrangement bullshit. His hearing was in the morning. Still time to jump on that redeye to D.C. But someone was Hoppin' Mad.

"When this is over, Lily, we need to talk."

Chapter Fourteen

On Thursday an infinitesimal ding in a Hopper frame set the lab in an uproar. With the gala a week away, nerves were frayed and the Objects Conservator and Angela got involved. Between calls with them and the lender, Lily checked her phone. Nothing from Paul. She opened C-SPAN on her computer. Guys in dark suits entered a hearing room. Matt stuck his head in her door: We need you. She logged out.

The ding took a tiny bit of filler and a dab of gilt. She returned to her office. On C-SPAN, senators were taking their seats. Still no Paul. Was this the right hearing? Maybe he was testifying later. Matt knocked to remind her about another meeting with Michel.

Lily sighed. Gina's final coup was set for the gala, but because of the exhibition gallery's physical constraints and the fact that it was a ticketed event, the micro-drama would be a photo op. Gina was playing up its surprise value for all it was worth, and not even Michel knew which Hopper it would be. That drove him nuts.

A ping: Sasha. *Hoppin' Mad sez I don't know Hopper!*

Lily texted back. *Friend of yours?*

Sasha. *Call me.*

But Matt was waving frantically. She was already late for Michel's meeting.

—

This time Michel offered neither coffee nor croissants.

"Come now, Gina," he wheedled, "which Hopper is it?" She smiled coyly. How often did she get to hold something over the director's head? He glanced direly at Lily. "Nobody here would dare reveal it."

"Perhaps not," Gina said, "but—"

"It could push the gala over the top." Michel appealed to his CMO. "Right, Pru?"

"Uh—" Pru said.

Lily's phone pinged. *Oxford Hotel 5 p.m.* James had come through with a heads-up. She texted Angela to meet her there and grinned at Gina. Gina frowned uncertainly.

"Put on your thinking cap, Pru!" Michel was saying. "How to use the final Hopper to promote the gala without identifying it in advance?"

"Um… an auction?" Pru said.

Michel frowned. Auctions were commercial. So—*American.*

"What if patrons bid on the opportunity to pose in the photo op?" Pru continued. "The bidding would be silent, of course…"

"…and we wouldn't need Offbeat," Gina said. "We can avoid any association with *Automat.*" She was warming to the idea. "We talk about the need to connect art to life, Michel. What better way than to allow patrons to be part of the final Hopper themselves?"

"Hmm." Michel steepled his fingers. "Stu?" he said to his CFO.

"The revenue from an auction would be negligible, but it adds nothing to the cost. Cutting out Offbeat also saves money. The real value's the intangible but incremental experiential—"

"Can I say something?" Lily asked.

Michel smiled ingratiatingly. "Of course."

"Vanessa Randall's killer is at large."

"And?" Michel said.

"Nothing happened at Civic Center Park, but—" Some nut in

Denver was Hoppin' Mad.

"Which proves there's no connection to Hopper." Michel's smile darkened. "Perhaps at Offbeat you were the jinx. Stu, Pru, Gina—brilliant idea. A silent auction at the gala for the privilege to pose in the final tableau."

———

"Who's Hoppin' Mad?" she asked Sasha on FaceTime.

"Some idiot who was at my lecture in Denver," Sasha fumed. "He had the gall to tell me I was wrong about Alta Hilsdale and Enid Saies!"

"Enid?"

"The girl engaged to the Frenchman with the waistcoat, the one who made Hopper bite off threads." Sasha clicked her teeth. "He claims she tried to get back with Hopper."

"Did she?"

Sasha hesitated. "Enid *did* break it off with the Frenchman.... But it was his tone, Lily. And the vile things he said about Alta. It went on for an entire screen, too graphic and hideous to repeat. He seems to take this personally, as if an affront to Hopper is an insult to himself."

Lily told her about Gina's caricatures. They seemed benign in comparison, but it was obviously the same guy. "Send me his screed."

"I was so furious, I deleted it!" Sasha sighed. "Probably a PhD candidate I was a little rough on eons ago. They follow you on social media and never forget a slight." She laughed ruefully. "The ivory tower isn't all it's cracked up to be, Lily. The overweening asses and cranks we encounter aren't just on the faculty."

"Watch your step, Sasha."

On screen, a girl in glasses came up behind Sasha and waved at Lily. Sasha brightened. "My TA, Kate—the real brains around here. We have a class."

Kate left and Sasha turned back to Lily.

"Yale's ivy is a garlic wreath. The only blood we ever spill is over tenure."

Chapter Fifteen

The Oxford Hotel had been renovated to preserve its illicit history and seedy charm. Mining union officers had been detained there before being whisked to Union Station to travel by train to Idaho to be tried for assassinating that state's governor. Its speakeasy bar had gone legit the day after Prohibition was repealed, but by the 1950s, The Oxford was a flophouse. Now tourists paid a premium to sleep a block from the Sixteenth Street Mall.

"Where the hell is Hopper?" Angela demanded.

In the lobby, tourists seemed more concerned about getting their wheelies from the deco tile floor up the narrow marble staircase to their rooms with clawfoot tubs.

"We're early," Lily reminded her. "We'll go to the Cruise Room later."

Pillars drew her eye to the balcony's wrought-iron railing. In the recess below, an upright piano stood against the wall. Rachel sat at its bench in a sleeveless red tea-length gown, with her hair demurely clasped at the nape of her neck and a finger idling a key. Was she killing time, or poised to strike a note to get the attention of Bo who, in his crisp shirt, vest and tie, hunched over a newspaper just feet away?

"*Room in New York!*" Lily exclaimed. The married couple glimpsed through the apartment window. As in the painting, Bo and Rachel were joined and separated by a small table to which a doily and bowl of fruit added a hint of domesticity and a pop of color. Dressed for an evening out, they ignored each other.

"Glad to see you too, dear," Angela muttered.

A plump girl in shorts came over to take a selfie with Bo. Her friend joined her. "Brad Pitt?" the second girl said. She took a selfie of all three of them. Giggling, they rejoined the tourists.

"They didn't even get it," Angela lamented. "Kids…"

Using The Oxford to establish the period was genius, and the recess evoked Hopper's cramped apartment at night. But there was no fruit bowl in the painting.

"Gina said the table looked incomplete—'What's a doily with nothing on top?'" Ernie had come up behind them, and he had Gina's nasal tone down pat. "Luckily the piano was here."

Rachel stretched, and Bo suppressed a sneeze.

"Five minutes," Ernie told them. The tourists had found the elevator, but walk-ins from the mall and well-heeled artsy types were filtering in with drinks from the bar. The clever simulation of an intimate flat drew them to the alcove under the stairs.

Bo reached for an apple.

"Don't you dare!" Ernie warned him.

"Just kidding," Bo said.

That fruit bowl wasn't just absent from Hopper's *Room in New York*; it was straight out of *Automat*. Did Gina realize that? Or maybe it was simply a bowl of fruit. Lily glanced at her watch. Paul's hearing must be over. She texted him. No reply. At the piano Rachel flexed her fingers, her image reflected in the glossy wood. Now Lily noticed another detail had been added: a pair of black gloves rested on the piano top.

Angela saw them too. "Tacky!" she loudly exclaimed.

Ernie blushed. "Some guest must've left them." But grabbing the gloves would only call attention to them, and the micro-drama was about to start. He raised his clapperboard.

Rachel softly struck a key.

A guy with a wineglass said, "What's this?"

Rachel trilled a scale and the lobby fell silent.

Ernie stepped to center stage and slammed the clapper.

"Edward Hopper, Take Three. Action!"

Rachel's hand moved silently across the keys, then struck a soft C. Bo kept reading the paper. She tapped the C again, louder. As Bo turned a page, two women in the audience exchanged a sympathetic look. Rachel banged the C together with a C sharp. Bo calmly reached for the apple. The crowd held its breath.

Rachel turned from the piano. "We'll be late for the exhibition," she told Bo.

He turned another page. "What's your hurry, dear? Last time we went to the museum, you were bored stiff."

An artsy woman nudged the guy with the wine, whom Lily now recognized as the director of The Museum of Contemporary Art. The audience was no longer walk-ins and tourists. Adapting to the intimacy of the couple in the apartment, they drew still closer.

"Because you were the artist, dear," Rachel said sweetly.

The artsy woman tittered.

Bo took a loud bite of his apple. "You used to like my paintings."

"Until you stole my palette and made it yours. And to think I introduced you to my gallery and got you your first commission!"

Bo sighed and set his paper down. He turned to the audience. "Should artists marry each other?"

The MCA director shouted, "Yes!"

Angela roared "No!"

The audience hooted.

Bo turned back to Rachel. "If only your paintings were a little more commercial, dear. Or, or … conceptual."

The director winced.

Rachel stood and pointed at the fruit. "Like duct-taping this banana to the wall?"

"Or meta…" Bo tried.

The director laughed uproariously.

Rachel grabbed an orange. "You want meta? I'll give you meta!"

Bo lifted his paper defensively. "I bet Edward Hopper never had to deal with this!"

The audience chanted, *Hop*-per! *Hop*-per!

Rachel waited for the crowd to hush. She looked from Bo to the orange and back again. Slowly her face lit. "You've given me an idea, darling. I'm going to my studio to paint!"

Bo cautiously emerged from his newspaper. "But what about the exhibition, dear? We have timed tickets…"

"You're right. Hopper can't wait." Rachel stepped to Bo's side. He rose and took her hand. Together they faced the audience. "And neither can you. Join us and Edward Hopper at The Denver Art Museum!"

They bowed and everyone burst into applause. The MCA director pounded Ernie on the back, and the actors were mobbed.

Lily looked around the lobby. Was the killer in the crowd?

If he was Hoppin' Mad, he'd been to Sasha's lecture and hadn't liked what she'd said about Alta Hilsdale and Enid Saies. Recreating *Hotel Room's* woman as Hopper's wife Jo would have rankled even more. She hoped the killer wasn't keeping score.

When she went to congratulate the troupe, the gloves were gone.

Chapter Sixteen

The Cruise Room's lighting was red, its artwork deco, and its martinis dirty. Lily half-expected *Misty* to be playing on the jukebox and Vanessa to strut naked across the bar.

"He's crushing on you," Angela said.

"Paul?"

"Ernie." Angela squinted at the drink menu. The rosy glow made it hard to read.

"We toured Offbeat the other night just so he could stick the knife in Cam and Laird."

"That little prick!" Angela laughed. "I should've known." She ordered herself a double martini and Lily a Singapore Sling. "Speaking of boys, I never got what you saw in that other kid—the docent trainee."

"Nick Lang?" When Angela's father was killed, she'd used Nick to distract her from Paul. She was still embarrassed about it. "A moment of madness."

"Horniness is more like it." Angela donned her half-glasses to read the food menu. "Whatever happened to him, anyway?"

"Nick? I think he left town." There'd been a For Sale sign on his house around the corner from her condo.

Oysters were out of season, so they ordered sliders and seafood escabeche. The bar was noisy; dirty martinis drew sophisticates, and small bites encouraged them to stay. While a well-heeled couple stopped to chat with Angela about renovations to the DCPA opera house, Lily texted Paul again. *Where R you?* Once Angela waved the couple away, Lily filled her in on what Paul had said about Laird.

"Starlet and director?" Angela said. "Golly gee! Even if the Kennedy Center bounced Laird for that or worse with a dozen Vanessa Randalls, predators like him just move down the line."

Maybe she was right. "And Cam?" Elena had said Angela knew him.

Angela hesitated. "We were in school together, a snotty little academy back East, which shall remain nameless."

"You and Cam?" Angela never discussed her conquests. "Tell me!"

"Kid stuff—and Cam is… trust me, he's harmless as they come. We lost touch till Offbeat was commissioned to stage Gina's microaggressions. He called and I put in a word."

"You got Cam the gig?" Lily asked.

"I was surprised he became a playwright," Angela admitted. "He was always bookish, but I thought he'd continue in art. He was a pretty decent illustrator."

"And?"

Angela shrugged. "I tossed him a bone for old time's sake, but Cam's no killer. My money's on Ernie. I don't buy his prissy little act, or his crap about art being details. Gimme a break!"

Lily laughed. "He'd be a great suspect if he didn't invite me backstage."

But Angela was on a tear. "He made us think the fruit was Gina's idea, like it had nothing to do with the riff or he'd ever let anyone else handle his precious sets! And speaking of details, leaving those tacky gloves on the piano was pretty damn sloppy." She finished her slider and signaled the waiter. Even on weeknights LoDo was a zoo, but she barely had to wave. Waitstaff all over town adored her. Lily glanced at her phone again.

"Paul?" Angela said.

"He wants me to move to D.C."

"That's one way to get out from under Michel's pointy little boot. Unless you want to come in-house with The Kurtz Foundation."

Lily looked up. "That's a lot of trust."

Angela laughed. "You already have my powers of attorney."

She'd scribbled her signature on a bunch of documents Angela gave her before their cross-country jaunt. Because Angela refused to fly in the company jet, The Foundation's lawyers had been pushing her to update her estate. *Damned if I'll let Michel or those pinstriped buzzards divvy up my carcass*, she'd said. Lily set down her slider and pushed back her plate.

"What's really eating you?" Angela said. "You weren't this worked up when George was killed. This isn't just about Vanessa Randall either, is it?"

Lily sighed. "I had dinner with Dad."

"Ah, yes." Angela set down her drink.

"Please, no psychoanalyzing."

"I'm not entirely blind, dear." She took off her glasses and reached for Lily's hand. "This is about your mom, right?"

Lily groaned. That cab ride back to the hotel after those martinis with The Whitney's curator. Nobody knew about the princess doll but Angela. Six months ago, when she was babbling drunk, how much else did she spill?

"Yeah, you talked about all of Hopper's unhappy blondes with satchels and valises," Angela continued. "Come on, kid. Your mom leaving, not looking you in the eye. Then her dying…"

What would she do without Angela, and why did she have to have such a damned good memory? "She wanted out!"

"And that was his fault?" Angela shook her head. "If we were doomed to be our parents, Lily, I'd be a prick like George…. Look, I'm no Freud, but isn't this about Paul?"

Where the hell was he?

"Afraid you'll drive him away, Lily? And speaking of Paul—"

"—we weren't—"

Ping. Lily grabbed her phone.

Gina. *Viva Las Vegas! Gala sold out!*

Bravo! she texted back. FU!

She'd had a choice. She could have stayed with Paul in that shack instead of dragging Dad out. *Where RU???* she texted Paul.

"—need to screw your head on straight, Lily. Your mom isn't Hopper's woman, and you need to forgive your dad." Angela squeezed her hand. "Most of all, you need to forgive yourself."

"What? It's too noisy to hear!"

Angela reached for her bag. "Let's get the fuck out of here."

—

This end of LoDo was restaurants and bars. As the cocktail crowd gave way to hardcore drinkers, music blared. Angela slipped in her stilettos, and Lily steadied her. They made it to the corner, but with the rush of oncoming pedestrians it was impossible to cross.

"Let's grab a cab," Lily said. A taxi bolted past.

"If we can get one to stop."

A raucous group tumbled out of a bar. One guy playfully pushed another. He shoved back. A girl laughed. Lily smelled beer and pot. Even without the Rockies losing another game, this wasn't the place to be. As an SUV ran the light, two men pounded on the windshield. It felt like they were pounding on her head.

"Damn these shoes." Angela's soles were slick, and she had a blister from a strap. She clutched Lily's arm. "So much for extra patrols. Where the hell are the cops?"

They were at the curb. "I'll call a Lyft." Lily got out her phone.

A red Jeep Grand Cherokee approached the intersection.

Lily's finger hovered over the Lyft app. Did Paul—

The Cherokee's engine gunned.

Jostled from behind, she lost her grip on Angela.

Angela stumbled on the curb. "Lily!"

Lily dropped her phone and tried to grab her. Moist hot breath tickled the back of her neck, closer than the crowd.

The Cherokee barreled towards the crosswalk.

She heard a grunt, felt a shove. Like a massive wave rebounding from a wall, Angela was torn from her grip.

She flew straight into the Cherokee's path.

Chapter Seventeen

"We sent flowers," Michel said solemnly. He gave Gina a little nod. "Gina saw to it that the array was stunning."

It was Friday morning. Brow furrowed, Michel sat at the head of his nearly empty conference table. At the opposite end a stack of hardbound exhibition catalogs towered, topped by a felt cloche.

"How is she?" Gina asked solicitously.

"Critical condition," Lily said.

"You were with her," Michel commiserated.

And all through the night. If she hadn't been looking at her fucking phone for a text from Paul—

"Nothing to do with that actress's death," Gina murmured.

"You were close," Michel said. *Were.* "Did she say anything—"

"She's in a fucking coma, Michel!" Lily cried.

He knitted his fingers. "Well, there's no doubt what she *would* say, correct?"

"That the show must go on?" Lily gripped the edge of the table.

"We all know how committed…" Gina trailed off.

Michel turned crisply to Gina. "You and Pru draft the release. Honored friend and patron, regrettable—*tragic*—accident, our hearts with her, etcetera. Greatest tribute is to forge on—"

"Cancel!" Lily shouted.

They turned to her in shock.

"He's here," she said.

"Who?" Michel said.

"The killer. He texted Sasha and Gina."

Gina shook her head vehemently.

"Spare us the drama, Mademoiselle," Michel agreed.

That grunt. The shove. "He feeds off Hopper."

Michel smirked. "No sane—"

"—and responsible museum would proceed with a show when there's a murder at the kickoff and its chief benefactor and patron has been thrown under a bus!"

"Bus?" Gina said.

"A fucking Jeep Grand Cherokee!"

"No need for profanity, Mademoiselle." Michel rose to his full five feet six inches. "You had every opportunity to convince us to postpone one week ago, after that poor actress's death."

"But I—"

"And now you have the gall to lecture me on moral obligations? You understand nothing. Canceling will only put the institution you claim to cherish at risk."

"What if he kills again?" Lily demanded.

Michel snorted. "If I were you, I'd be more concerned about Angela. You'd better hope she lives." He swiveled to Gina. "I want that release out within the hour." He turned back to Lily. "And you, Mademoiselle, have a question of your own to answer."

Who cared about his questions? Angela's blood was on her hands.

"Do you want to keep your fucking job?" he said.

—

On her way out, she texted Sasha.

Come.

Chapter Eighteen

Paul was leaning against her door, scrolling through his phone.

"Paul!"

He looked up with a start. His pinstripe suit had held its press but his eyes were dark smudges. "Where've you been, Lily?"

"No, where have *you* been? I've been texting and calling…What are you doing here?"

Paul smiled crookedly. "It was my turn."

She set down her purse and went to him. "Where's my flowers?"

"The florists were closed when I landed."

Sandalwood and cloves. More gray in his hair?

"Do I get a kiss or what?" he asked.

She touched his cheek. Hint of stubble. Her hand moved to his chest. Smooth and taut—he'd been working out. Was he healed enough to swim? Through the shirt his skin felt hot. How long had it been? Too long—he leaned down and kissed her.

"You taste like vodka," she said.

"Plane." He kissed her more deeply. She let it linger.

She unlocked the door and he sank onto her couch. Jack sniffed

Paul's hand-tooled Oxfords, then jumped up beside him. He'd clawed the hell out of Nick, but now he rolled over for a belly rub. He didn't even do that for Dad.

Paul loosened his tie. "At least someone's in my corner."

"Where's your bag?" she said.

"The Westin." When George Kurtz was murdered, it was The Ritz—but that was on the FBI's dime. When Paul came to see her, he stayed at her condo. "I may be here awhile, didn't want to impose."

"Impose?" Lily said.

"I heard about Angela. Is she—"

"What happened at the hearing?"

"I quit the FBI." He started untying his shoes.

"What!" she exclaimed.

"I'm joining a Denver firm."

"Paul, the FBI's your career!"

He gave a short laugh. "You'd be surprised at the demand for ex-agents with white-collar expertise."

"I told you I'd consider moving—"

"Now you don't have to decide." He rose. "I'm too tired to fight, Lily. Mind if I stay?"

He took off his jacket and draped it on the bedroom chair. She turned off the light and came up behind him. Her hands reached under his shirt and stopped at the ropy scar.

"Do I need a letter from my doctor?" Paul said lightly. Kurtz's killer had nicked his aorta. The FBI medevacked him to a trauma center and cracked open his sternum. He'd been on the table nine hours before they wheeled him out, and even then it was touch and go.

He switched on the bedside lamp. "You have to look at it sometime."

She turned away.

"It's that repulsive?" he said.

"No."

He yanked open his shirt. She caught a glimpse—red, livid, angry. Her fault.

"What the fuck does it take?" he said.

"I'm sorry..."

He stood and buttoned his shirt.

"Don't go."

"Oh, I'm staying. Just not here."

"Please—"

He put on his jacket and kissed her forehead. "I need a shower and a shave."

"You can have the bed."

He snorted. "Without you?"

"Tomorrow's Saturday. We can sleep in, and I'll give you a private tour—"

He tied his shoes. "I'll see you at the lab."

Chapter Nineteen

"When's the last time you slept?" Johnson asked.

It was never too late for a drink at the rumpled DPD detective's favorite cop dive. "Wild sex, eh?" he continued.

"What?" Paul said.

"Your top button's missing."

"When's the last time that tie of yours saw the cleaner's?" Paul said.

"Either—"

"Please."

"—that little blonde tore off your shirt or—"

"Hate to disappoint you."

"—she kicked you out!"

"You get the prize." Paul signaled for another round of boilermakers.

"Can't say I blame her," Johnson said. "You look like shit."

"Thanks. Any leads on Vanessa Randall?"

Johnson looked wounded. "What about you?"

"Laird Bennett—"

"A tip from the blonde?"

"Her name's Lily, as you damn well know. You grilled her long enough after Vanessa Randall was killed." Their drinks came with a bowl of hardboiled eggs. Paul shook his head. Denver had interesting bar food.

"Cops need protein," Johnson said defensively.

"Just give me the photos."

Johnson slid a manila folder across the table.

Paul started with the wound. A long oblique incision to the neck. Deepest under the left ear, then tailing off and down to the right. No hesitation marks or defensive wounds. "Left to right from behind," he said. Cuts from the front were short and angled, and there'd be more than one stab. "No struggle or signs she moved after the attack. With a cut carotid you can flail for ten minutes. He restrained her head. It was pretty damn quick."

Johnson peeled him an egg. "Pro?"

Paul shook his head again. "They target the brainstem from the back of the neck, or the aorta from behind the collarbone. That takes precision, strength, and speed."

"Rage?" Johnson asked. "Sex?"

"No mutilation or overkill," Paul said.

"That rules out Andy Bragg."

Lily thought the killer made Vanessa dress before he cut her throat. And wouldn't a pissed-off ex stab her from the front? But Paul wasn't quite ready to rule the obvious suspect out. "Bragg was in the military, right?"

"Washed out of the Seals."

"But he'd learn a silent kill." He turned to a photo of the table with the cup. "Odd."

"What?" Johnson asked.

"No spray—did he catch the blood? And why bother?" Paul pushed the photos back. "To let him get that close, she must've known him."

Johnson winced and stood. "Call of nature." He headed in the direction of the john.

Paul looked at his phone. A dozen texts in the last twenty-four hours from Lily. *Where are you? R U OK? When R U—* It had all happened so fast. He shook his head. He should've texted her, told her he was coming. Now everything was fucked up.

Johnson plopped a McDonald's bag on the scarred wooden table.

Paul reached for a burger. "I didn't take you for a mother hen."

"They obviously don't feed you in D.C." Johnson said.

"How many times were you married?"

"Three."

Paul wolfed the burger down. "You should've had kids."

"Who needs them when I got you?" Johnson gave him his burger and fries. "Why are you really here?"

"I quit the FBI. Walked out after a Senate hearing."

"Oh, yeah?"

"Admin's not for me."

Johnson guffawed, but his pouched eyes showed concern.

"I mean it," Paul said.

"No offense, but we know what happened last time you were in the field."

"Ouch."

Johnson snagged a fry. "Nick Lang moved. He's off the radar."

Paul set his burger down. "I couldn't care less—"

"You cared enough to bust Lang's nose and break into his house. What's on that thumb drive you stole?" Damned if he'd let Nick hold that and the illegal search of his home over him forever. "Maybe he didn't kill George Kurtz—"

If only he had!

"—but you humiliated him, Paul. I know Nick's type—"

Paul pushed his plate away. "And here I thought I was doing you a favor."

"Nick knows you'd do anything for her, and he's squirrelly enough to set you up. And you're just obsessed enough—"

Paul rose. "Lang's got nothing on me."

"So help me God, Paul, nothing better happen—"

Paul threw some bills on the table. "By the way, your weapon's a razor."

Chapter Twenty

Driving to The Westin, Paul replayed that morning's hearing.

Dressed in their Sunday best and clutching legal pads and briefing folders, bright-faced interns had filed into the Senate chamber with the gargantuan American flag. Behind the horseshoe-shaped dais, a wall of marble, blotched like a Rorschach, soared. In the center was an enormous U.S. Senate seal with a slot for a camera. Paul had straightened his tie— her silk Armani. This wasn't his first rodeo.

Staffers set out bottles of water. A bearded guy in sneakers and scruffy jeans tested the microphones. The three rows behind Paul were roped for witnesses' relatives and special visitors. In back was a bullpen for the press. The room was filling up; FBI directors were appointed for ten years. He looked at his watch. Five minutes.

This wasn't about him, it was about Mark.

A door behind the dais opened and senators filtered in with their aides. The matronly one from Minnesota. The Utah popinjay who patted his sleek silver hair when the camera pointed his way. South Carolina brushing crumbs from his camel-haired lapel. Spittle flecked Iowa's cracked lips, and Paul resisted the urge to reach for water.

Not so much as a damn parking ticket.

But this hearing wasn't about Mark either. One side would lob softballs and make folksy asides about growing up in God's country or on a farm. The other would pose gotchas from the search-and-seizure case the Supreme Court had decided that morning. Which senator would lean forward cozily and ask, but what's he *really* like? Paul knew the drill: answer all questions with Mark's single-minded devotion to the law. They didn't know Mark's wife had been diagnosed with breast cancer and he didn't plan to serve out his term. You're next in line, kid.

Paul's scar itched. Not just his scar. On his desk sat a FISA warrant for the phone records of a Tadjik truckdriver who was right now driving down the New Jersey Turnpike, and a top-level confidential informant was coming in this afternoon. Paul's brush with death had vaulted him to a top-level supervisory role, but since George Kurtz's murder, white-collar firms had courted him coast-to-coast. Why anyone thought he'd be interested in a desk job—what the hell was he doing here? In his pinstriped suit, with the camera in the Senate seal pointed at him, he felt like a Yorkie mix at the Westminster Dog Show.

Two more senators entered. Louisiana with the courtly drawl and alligator grin, the junior from Utah beady-eyed and mirthless. The chamber was cold but sweat trickled down the back of Paul's neck. Without windows you couldn't tell day from night, and the noise-muffling acoustics and sheer scale of the place made it feel like a postmodern nightmare he couldn't wake up from.

He tightened his tie. The knot slipped on the silk. Lily had given it to him the night before she found out about his wife. It had taken him ten damn years—and George Kurtz's murder—before she spoke to him again. If getting stabbed in the heart had taught him one thing, it was not to waste time. What would it take to get her to move to D.C.? More than dope on why the Kennedy Center axed Laird Bennett, or an opening at the Phillips.

The chamber buzzed softly. He stole another backwards glance.

He'd wanted her to come. To show her how a farm boy from Iowa could handle the bright lights of a Senate chamber as well as a crazy killer in a dirty shack. And then take her out on the town and show her what she was missing in Denver. If Hopper was a hit, and with Angela Kurtz as her patron, she could write her own ticket. Would she like that townhouse in Georgetown, or the DuPont Circle condo with a real balcony?

He laughed to himself. What the hell was he thinking?

Trust her to sabotage all she'd worked for by getting mixed up in another damn murder! Of course she thought it was about Hopper; what else would a conservator— especially her—think? But there was something hinky about it. Johnson had e-mailed him the preliminary reports. That alcove was pretty damn tight. If it was Laird Bennett or Andy Bragg, it took real stones to do it with a hundred people outside the door... The murmuring stopped.

Senator Susan Grace strode in. In her signature red suit and carrying a Starbucks cup, she caught Paul's eye and winked before taking her seat at the center of the dais.

He straightened his tie again.

Just get this over with.

A couple of colleagues came over to Grace to chat. Paul looked at his statement. Instead he saw the autopsy report. The killer's precision was chilling. Single incision, perfectly timed and placed... Something else about the timing. Another murder, on the eve of Lily's show? The sweat on the back of his neck was cold.

Get her to D.C. before she gets hurt.

He took a deep breath.

At least Nick Lang was out of the picture—that grinning prick. Maybe he didn't kill Kurtz, but he'd fucked Lily and recorded it. He heard Nick taunt him when he came back with Johnson and the warrant. Felt Nick's face crunch, saw his nose gush red as his hair, heard him swear through broken teeth, *It's not over.* Johnson was too smart to ask, and all Lily knew was Nick disappeared. But Paul had the thumb drive. Come to think of it...

The senators were taking their seats.

As a suspect in Vanessa Randall's murder, Nick made a crazy kind of sense. More than Laird Bennett or Andy Bragg. Bennett was a heavy breather, and Bragg didn't have the wits or patience to pull it off. Lang, on the other hand, was a planner. Just look at that tape and see how he channeled rage… Paul laughed uneasily. Bad as her, seeing things that weren't there. What she really needed was protection from herself.

No matter what a hit Hopper was, they'd never let her leave the lab. And her scheming old man… Fuck the FISA warrants and the Tadjik truckdriver! His deputy would handle the CI. The minute this dog-and-pony show was over he'd grab those condo brochures, some dried shrimp for her cat, and a plane.

Taptaptap.

The AV tech rechecked Paul's mic and gave Senator Grace a thumb's up. She set down her Starbucks cup. When she'd sent him to Denver to bird-dog George Kurtz's case, he'd thought it was because she smelled the farm on him, had thought she was kidding when she said someday Mark's job would be his. But he wasn't for sale. Afterwards, that nicked aorta came in handy. Everybody loved a hero…. The press took their seats, and there was a stir as visitors made way for a latecomer. Paul glanced over his shoulder again. Average guy in sport coat and tie, lanyard with a pea-green pass. His back was turned as he gestured apologetically to the people around him. Something familiar—

The dais was a tier of faces. Grant cleared her throat.

Paul looked back again.

The nose was off-kilter, his auburn hair shorn. He grinned at Paul.

You.

Grant rose to administer the oath.

The man reached up as if to scratch his left ear.

"Assistant Deputy Director Reilly?" Grant said.

Nick Lang cocked his finger at Paul and drew it left-to-right across his throat.

Chapter Twenty-One

The light from the screen bathes you in its glow. Wherever you turn, women flirt. They don't interest you. They're not The Girl.

You log into the chatroom.

Your friends, the guys. All walks of life—you'd be surprised. You know them by their handles. You change yours, but by whatever name you go, they know you. You steer clear of the hard stuff. It can be traced and you don't need it anyway. You have films of your own, not like some of these guys. You've had sex with a woman—of course you did! But Vanessa was different, with her it wasn't about sex. *Thanks so much for your little gift… Sorry I can't see you tonight. Maybe Tuesday—or Thursday afternoon?* And Angela. *Such tacky gloves!* Who the fuck did they think they were screwing with?

Tonight the guys are worked up over a video that's gone big. You click on the link.

Lunch hour on a midtown street. Men in hard hats unwrap deli subs. Hoodies under jackets and steam from thermoses says it's cold. The camera pans to a McDonald's with office workers streaming in and out, then back to the hard hats at the construction site.

Enter a girl and boy. He's in a pea jacket and wool watch cap, she's in a red puffer coat with a fur-trimmed hood and foxy stiletto boots. A hard hat whistles soundlessly and scratches his crotch. His friends laugh. The Boy says something to Puffer Girl. She shakes her head. They walk faster. Life is better on mute.

You've seen this guy's work. Solid instinct for drama, milks the anticipation, gives the scene room to unfold. Anonymity is his reward— with Vanessa, yours was better. *Fuck Tuesday night!* Unlike Hopper, you will not beg.

The camera cuts to Puffer Girl and The Boy in a store window, then back to the street. He takes her arm. She shakes him off. A gust ruffles her hood, and she defiantly raises her pointy little chin. Three steps behind, he calls after her. She pulls out her phone and starts texting. *Sorry I couldn't make it... so busy these days!* Not too busy to jerk him around. Or for a visit with a razor.

Two gals with shopping bags exit the store. Seeing The Boy and Puffer Girl, they whisper. A moment of recognition, the stuff that unites strangers. A slice of urban life that becomes an anecdote later—*I know just how she felt!* They nod understandingly to Puffer Girl. Funny how someone else's misery makes you feel good. The camera tracks the shoppers to the curb. They hail a cab. Bit players exiting stage left. Brilliant.

Back to The Boy. His cap makes his head comically round—funny-looking kid, his script from birth. And whose fault was that but his mom's? She probably made promises too, ones she didn't keep. *Get out there, run a few laps, everything will be fine. You'll find the one...* On the screen, a gent with good hair and a briefcase passes. Looking back and seeing Puffer Girl striding down the sidewalk three paces ahead of The Boy, he shrugs sympathetically. Hey kid, we've all been there. He keeps on walking. So much better without sound. Or words.

The Boy recedes, an epilogue to his own drama, as the camera tracks Puffer Girl. Her heart-shaped face fills the screen. She smiles—laughs. Unaware of the camera, she exits the frame. The Boy rubs his head.

Suddenly he smashes it into the window.

What does it take?

You were careful with Vanessa. Hopper would understand the gloves, but was it too obvious to leave another pair at The Oxford? You meant them for Lily, but Angela ruined it by butting in. She had no idea who she was fucking with! And that riff about Hopper stealing Jo's palette was out of control; he would not have been pleased. But there's more Hoppers to come.

You log into the discussion board. Messages immediately start coming.

Where you been, Hoppin' Mad?

Your new name. *Away. Back now.*

A reply. *Poor bastard, eh?*

You tap. *Gladiators all.*

Another. *But you said the game's rigged!*

You tap again.

Till the right one comes along.

Chapter Twenty-Two

Saturday was a free day at the museum. Groups lined up in the atrium lobby for tours, local artists demonstrated watercolor technique in the paint studio, and the kids summer day camp had just started. Dodging retirees with water bottles and fanny packs, Lily and Paul mounted the grand staircase to the exhibition gallery on the second floor. The Hopper show didn't open for a week, and final touches were being made.

At the entrance, workers were installing an immense opaque screen of Hopper's *Nighthawks*. The painting itself wasn't in the show; a so-called "immovable," it was simply too important for The Art Institute of Chicago to lend. But it was Hopper's most iconic work, and in homage to him, the show's designers wanted to throw visitors ever-so-slightly off-balance by recreating a noirish, convivial mood. Lily had to admit the screen was magnificent.

Viewed through a plate glass window and lit from within by cold fluorescent lights, the customers in Hopper's all-night diner shared the counter but nothing else. The redhead had a sandwich, her male companion a coffee cup, and the man a few stools away a cigarette. Hopper hadn't painted a door, and the screen was being mounted directly over the gallery's entrance. Upon arrival, gala guests would be greeted by a human counterman in a white jacket and peaked hat.

"Where everybody knows your name," Paul said testily.

"I invited you to stay," she reminded him.

"At least I slept." The whiff of chlorine said he'd also swum laps. Even with the circles under his eyes and the new gray in his hair, he still looked good in a T-shirt and Levi's.

The gallery had been repartitioned almost unrecognizably for the show. So as not to upstage Hopper's muted primary colors, the new walls were mauve, periwinkle, and dove gray. Gina's assistant was in intense conversation with Kip about the placement of a display case containing a laminated diner menu, a *Life Magazine* with Marilyn Monroe on the cover, and a maroon military-style cap worn by 1940s theater usherettes.

"The girl in *New York Movie* didn't wear a hat," Paul pointed out.

"Very good!" Lily said. "Still betting on Andy Bragg, or has Laird Bennett moved up your list?"

"Neither." He peered warily around a partition.

"Gina doesn't come in this early on Saturday."

"Thank God." She'd never gotten the full story of what had happened between them during the Kurtz investigation, but it was on the long list of things for which Gina was always paying her back. The Phillips was sounding better all the time.

In the last room, a sheet of glass leaned on a scaffold waiting to be framed. Behind it, James fiddled with something big and green. He waved at Lily. Ernie looked up from working on the frame. Seeing her and Paul, he gave it an extra hard whack. Lily introduced them.

Paul pointed to the thing behind the scaffold. "Beached whale?"

Ernie quickly signaled James to cover it with a tarp. "Gina will have my head if I spoil the surprise."

"Surprise?" Paul shook his head. "Continuing to stage these little dramas is insane!"

Ernie glanced at James. "One more before the gala." Lowering his voice, he appealed to Lily. "Nothing happened at the last two. And does anyone care about Vee? They let Andy go, and nobody's questioned Cam or Laird."

"How do you know?" Paul asked.

Ernie snorted. "There's no secrets backstage. My money's on Laird." He hesitated. "The girls are scared of him."

"And Cam?" Lily asked.

"He made Vee strip." He looked like he wanted to say more.

James had pulled out a sandwich and was settling down on a sawhorse to eat. Ernie looked at him disdainfully, but maybe he'd say more over his own steak frites at Atelier. "Have lunch with us," she said, "my treat."

Ernie shook his head and reached for his hammer. He struck a resounding blow. "Someone's got to make the trains run."

—

Angela had adored Atelier's escargots, the owner toiling in the open kitchen, and the waiter with the boat-necked striped shirt. Now they looked at Lily mournfully.

"How is Madame?" the waiter asked.

"I'll tell her you asked."

The owner sent over a bottle of wine and a pâté on the house. Today's special was rabbit.

"Is Angela still in intensive care?" Paul asked Lily.

"I don't know why he went after her, but—"

"That's a big *if*."

"It was no accident." She filled Paul in about Gina's caricatures and Sasha's text, but left out the gloves and fuck-me's; he'd have a field day with those. "I'm picking Sasha up at the airport tomorrow."

Paul frowned. "I didn't realize they were that close."

"Just a short visit. She has to be back Tuesday for a symposium."

His frown deepened. "Not planning anything stupid, are you?"

"With a Yale art history professor?"

He set down his drink. "Look, Lily, seeing patterns is your game.

Sometimes they're real and sometimes they're not. Your dad—"

Pivot. "It's time you two met."

"We did. It was in a shack—"

"For dinner." What had she just said? Too late to take it back—and she owed it to Angela. If she hadn't been obsessing over a text from Paul, she might have seen that SUV coming. She had to get her head on straight. "Tuesday night?"

"Okay."

The waiter brought Lily's salmon and Paul's rabbit in mustard sauce.

"Speaking of patterns," she said, "have you looked at Laird Bennett's personnel file?"

He started deboning the rabbit. "It's under seal."

Which meant something was there. She'd eventually get it from him, but meantime she had to eliminate Cam. Maybe call him for a drink. "Coming over tonight?"

Paul stared into his wine. "Johnson's taking me to a Rockies game. A double-header."

"Johnson?" She snorted. "Ernie's right, he's not—"

"I saw him look at you." He set the bones neatly on the bone plate. "Don't lead him on."

"Ernie?" She laughed. "I would if he'd give me a heads-up on the flash mobs." Paul wasn't laughing. "Seriously, Paul, his love objects have to sit still."

"Poor rabbit." Paul raised his fork. "I'd steer clear."

Chapter Twenty-Three

The East was on hospital row and uptown from the law firms on Seventeenth. The young professionals to which it catered appreciated the short-term rentals with Internet in the lobby, common spaces with espresso machines, and pet spa with a dog wash. Paul's last unofficial act at the FBI had been tracking Nick Lang there.

Before he met up with Lily at the museum, he'd watched Nick drive off in his Audi Cabriolet. A lot fancier than the old pickup he used to drive. But Nick was all about appearances. Was the Audi rented too? Paul told the kid at the glassed-in leasing office in the lobby he was in town for a patent trial and requested a tour.

The East knew its demographic. Units were unfurnished, but a rental company it worked with had the floorplans. To get tenants to hang out, there was a gym and outdoor pool. Upper units offered park and mountain views, and there was even a Zen garden. Units were soundproof, plantation blinds ensured privacy, and a studio apartment was cheaper than The Westin. The Welcome Packet included a gift certificate for ClusterTruck, the latest in food delivery.

"Hit-or-miss," the kid confided, "but the ahi tuna salad's good." He scanned a new-age fob key on the pad at a door. "These fobs are the only access to units and amenities, and to the building from the street or the garage after 10:00 p.m."

"Nifty," Paul said. "What's the catch?"

He frowned innocently. "Catch? What do you mean, Mr.—"

"Custer. Where does all that data go?"

"We need to know tenants' whereabouts to ensure they obey the rules."

Hello, Big Brother. "Rules?"

"Pool closes at 10:00." They were alone, but the kid lowered his voice discreetly. "Medical personnel work crazy shifts. God knows why you'd swim at 2:00 in the morning, but neighbors complain. What law firm did you say you're with?"

Paul's smile was almost as good as a badge. "Show me a townhouse."

Nick had signed a three-month townhouse lease. With a private garage and direct street access, a townhouse was perfect for flying under the radar. Whatever his plans were in Denver, they wouldn't take long.

The display unit faced Nick's, which made them mirror images. The cavernous space had a vaulted ceiling and narrow stairs to a sleeping loft. Track lighting softened the effect, but Paul saw Nick's smirk play across the wall. Come and get me… He wasn't looking over his shoulder forever for that slimy prick.

Now it was evening, and he sat on a bench with a carton of Thai watching Nick's townhouse. He had interviews lined up next week, but he'd done the big firm scene, had enough with admin and bureaucracy. A white-collar practice belonged in a lean, mean litigation boutique like the one that had been chasing him since Kurtz's murder. But he was more concerned about Lily's future than his. What was she doing tonight?

Not going out—she'd invited him over before he said he was going to a Rockies game. Maybe dinner with her old man. Harry Sparks, still with his games. Her choosing her dad in that filthy shack had been the right thing to do; if you weren't loyal to your folks, who could you be loyal to? Paul's scar itched but he didn't let himself scratch it. It was ugly—he saw that every morning in the mirror. But that wasn't why she was afraid of it. What would he say to Harry tomorrow night? Let your daughter go?

A light blinked on in Nick's townhouse. Nick stood at the window. Skinny, wired, jacked—not like that little rabbit with the big leather toolbelt, giving that poor little nail an extra hard whack. Did Nick see him? He hoped so. The plantation blinds closed except for a slit. The condo light went off.

Now a white light bounced off the empty walls. Computer screen. The one thing that prick wasn't doing was playing his sex tape of Lily— the thumb drive was in Paul's pocket, and if Nick had made a copy, neither of them would be here now. Even if he wasn't Vanessa Randall's killer, so long as he was in Denver he was a threat to Lily. But he must know Paul wouldn't show her the tape either.... The computer went off and track lighting illuminated Nick's progress up the stairs to the loft. Apparently he was in for the night. Paul threw away the takeout and got into his rental car.

He had just one question for Nick.

Why did you lure me here?

Chapter Twenty-Four

The waitress rushed past with a tray of drinks and a thousand-yard stare.

"Thanks for meeting me," Lily told Cam. He'd suggested this place on the Sixteenth Street Mall. It was hard to get a table on Saturday night, but they'd found one near the bar.

"Angie's an old friend," Cam said, and shook his head mournfully. There was something shabbily professorial about him, with the walrus moustache and belly bulging comfortably over the frayed waistband of his corduroys. "Pity they don't allow visitors in the ICU."

"She told me you met at school."

"Did she?" Cam waved at the waitress. "Angie didn't deserve to be thrown—"

Thrown?

"—under a bus." The waitress went in the other direction.

"A Jeep Cherokee."

"Whatever. Of course, with those ridiculous shoes…"

"Shoes?" How would he know which ones Angela wore that day?

"Stilettos, right?" Cam said. "She slipped, I suppose."

"You don't think so?"

His wattles shook. "After Vee? Please."

Cam signaled the waitress again. The joint was hopping, but she seemed to deliberately avoid them as she juggled drinks and plates from the 1940s-style diner window across the floor. He seemed comfortable here, maybe even a regular. He waved more insistently.

"Why them?" Lily said.

"Vee got around, and you know Angie. Don't take this wrong, but she could be kind of a... ballbreaker, don't you think?" He sighed theatrically. "And I a sweaty-palmed neurotic boy."

It was impossible to imagine him with Angela, but he did have an oily charm. She could see him bringing actresses gifts. "Neurotic—you?"

"To say nothing of sweaty palms."

Their waitress had taken a break to chat with the bartender, who ignored them too. But Angela had tossed him a bone... "You're a playwright," Lily said. Cam stopped waving at the waitress. "*Summer Evening* at the park and *Room in New York* at The Oxford were brilliant."

He looked at her with new interest. "Hopper's a dramatist's dream. You can read into his paintings whatever you want."

So he knew Hopper's other works. "I heard Rachel did some improv..."

"In the spirit of the role." He'd been at the park, too.

"How'd you decide to make her a Valley Girl?"

His eyes glinted. "The script wrote itself."

"And Hopper's wife, Jo at The Oxford?"

"The eternal battle of the sexes." He tried getting the waitress's attention again. "A playwright thinks of roles, or types. I asked myself, what does A Girl Like Her want?"

"And Vee?"

Cam leered, but his moustache made it look silly. No wonder Angela and the waitress didn't take him seriously. Did Vanessa?

"I especially liked your bit with the gloves," she continued. "In *Automat*—"

"The gloves were Laird's idea. The kid—"

"Ernie?"

"He said there should be one. Laird insisted on two."

"Why?" she asked.

"To prolong the tease!"

She tried again to picture a teenage Cam trying to get to first base with Angela, but the image just wouldn't come. *A snotty little academy which shall remain nameless*, she'd said. The adolescent fumbling Angela had hinted at had been enough to remember and be embarrassed about all these years later, and to make her toss him a bone. But he seemed so out of her league. "What's the next one, Cam?"

"Gina won't tell you?" He relented. "A hint: it's a monologue. And this time, Rachel better not improvise."

The waitress finally arrived.

"What can I get you, sir?" Her perky smile stopped at her eyes.

"Come now." He fiddled with his hanky. "Do I look that old?"

She winked. "Show me what you got later, handsome. Your date looks thirsty."

"Two pale ales."

"You got it, slugger."

He grinned, and the waitress drew back.

Sweaty palms were the least of it.

Cam's incisors were ground to nubs.

Chapter Twenty-Five

Patios are for tourists. The real action's inside.

From your table by the bar, you take in the scene. The frowning bodybuilder pumping suds, the waitress with the silky ponytail. Tonight the script changes.

After making you wait long enough, she slaps down your pint of ale.

"Sorry!" She flips her ponytail and pulls the dishrag from her waistband. She wipes up the spill and gives you a fresh cocktail napkin. Her lipstick is orange-pink—persimmon, not Vanessa's scarlet. You have Ponytail's color in your pocket.

Hips swaying, Ponytail moves to the next table and leans in to take the order. Solo guy, nothing special—a what-the-fuck. Not pumped like the bartender, but enough to rate an extra moment. Ponytail brushes WTF's arm. He says something that makes her smile, and she rewards him by sweeping back her hair. Her shirt gapes to reveal a hint of seafoam-colored bra. Then she sways off.

You scan the room. Who's a player? Guy hunched over a cocktail in the booth by the wall. Shades give away more than they hide, like him ogling the chesty redhead with the stiff in chinos by the door—lawyer slumming on Saturday night. Bit player. Is the star Shades—or Red?

Red swivels forty-five degrees to show her legs. She likes being watched. You freeze the frame. No camera tonight, just when you're in the shot. You sip slowly, letting the negative ion energy build like it's been doing since Vanessa. But you're in no hurry. You have all night, time to set up the kill shot right. The point is to stay loose and limber, amuse yourself, stay on the game. You let off some steam with Angela and Gina and Yale—negative ion energy has to go somewhere. Because if there's one thing you don't want to blow, it's your thing with Lily.

Ponytail prances to the bar. She arches her back, disguising it with a yawn like she's tired. The bartender is a sullen muscle-bound pumped-up jerk like Andy Bragg, and almost as pretty. She touches Prettyboy's hand. You imagine her fingers lingering on yours. Prettyboy's surliness fades and his lips purse in a soundless whistle. Last call is less than an hour.

You freeze the frame. Stop the clock. Retard the moment. You can make her final moment like Vanessa's. But you want more. To be touched like Prettyboy? To have a girl like Ponytail want you?

Ponytail is back, her smile as empty as your glass. "One for the road, slugger?"

You shake your head. She thinks it's that easy? Something flits across her face. Regret? Maybe you're imagining it, but it makes you wonder. Do you have this all wrong? You lock eyes. She looks so—

She picks up your glass and turns away.

What would the chatroom say? They like your advice. It's practical but extreme—a bit out there, even for them. You never ask theirs. But if you did, what would you say?

There's this gorgeous barmaid. She has the hots for a bartender—you know the type. No brains, all brawn. She doesn't see or doesn't care. But I can make her love me. Must I beg? Or should I—

Ponytail serves WTF, then gestures to Prettyboy and points in the direction of the ladies' room. Dilemma resolved. No need for advice. You know what you're going to do. And what the guys would say.

Go for it, Hoppin' Mad!

You put the cocktail napkin in your pocket and rise. You wave to Prettyboy, who waves back. Good customer—a regular—signing off on Saturday night. You won't be back.

You follow Ponytail to the john. You take the door marked Gents. A guy is at the urinal. You enter a stall and scribble on the napkin. You take your time adding a personal flourish, and then a persimmon smear. How long will it take Prettyboy to figure out what Ponytail's lipstick and your own sticky mark on a napkin mean after five minutes in a john together?

The guy at the urinal leaves. You exit the stall and listen at the wall. Toilet in the ladies' room flushes. Water runs in a sink. *All Staff Please Wash Your Hands!* You take a crisp twenty-dollar bill from your wallet and fold it in the napkin. You leave the men's room just as Ponytail emerges from the ladies.

You bump her shoulder. She turns.

"Oh!" she says. "I didn't see you."

Of course not.

"Do me a favor?" You slip her the folded napkin. "Tip the bartender."

Ponytail goes to the bar and gives Prettyboy the napkin. He opens it with a smile. Seeing what's inside, Prettyboy startles and drops it like it's radioactive. What, he never saw a girl's lipstick mixed with negative ion energy before? He grabs Ponytail's arm. What the fuck? he mouths.

She shakes her head and tries to pull away. Prettyboy brandishes the napkin. She rears back, then turns and points. You smile and wave. Prettyboy jerks her arm and shouts.

Cut.

And print.

Chapter Twenty-Six

Lily switched off the late news. The Rockies had lost both games in their double-header and Paul and Johnson would be sudsing their sorrows. She couldn't wait to pick up Sasha tomorrow. Too antsy to sleep, she replayed her drinks with Cam. Angela was right, he was pathetic. Not just the sweaty palms, but those teeth. And his bit about Laird insisting on two gloves—was it to cast suspicion on him? There was that pair left on the piano at The Oxford. Angela had loudly called them tacky—maybe that provoked the killer to attack her. Or maybe the gloves meant something else altogether.

She opened her laptop and began scrolling through Hopper's paintings looking for ones with women who wore gloves. Secretaries, shop girls, usherettes, guests in hotel lobbies... *Automat* was the only one. But now she noticed something else. Hopper's men aged, but with rare exceptions, his women seemed frozen in their late twenties to mid-thirties. If Jo insisted on being his only model so she'd never age, that made sense. But their faces were out of synch with their bodies and attire.

In *Summer Evening*, the boy's T-shirt and pleading posture registered youth; but despite her bandeau and shorts, the girl seemed older—hard-faced and sullen. In *Room in New York*, the man's tie and vest and the way he hunched over his paper suggested maturity; take the wife out of that evening dress and she could be the same age as the girl on the porch or the flapper or the hard-faced stripper in *Girlie Show*. In the paintings of couples, what signified marriage was their ignoring each other.

Lily clicked on Elizabeth Griffiths Smith's portrait again. This time she looked past the sunken eyes and unsmiling lips, to the lower part of the composition. Hopper's mother's purple taffeta sleeves were pushed back from her wrists. Her bony forearms sagged, and a bracelet hung loosely. Veined hands clutched the fabric of her skirt, the knuckles swollen and arthritic. Hopper's depiction of his mother's face was unsparing and cruel, but the hands were painted with such loathing…

Sasha pinged. *C U 2morrow!*

It was past midnight, but Yale professors and art conservators weren't the only ones who were up.

—

A top-heavy bouquet of roses and gladioli wilted at the ICU station. The card read, *Get well soon from your DAM friends!*

"Angela Kurtz?" Lily asked the charge nurse.

"Ms. Kurtz has a traumatic brain injury." She kept reading charts. "No visitors."

"I was with her when it happened."

The nurse looked up. "Sorry, dear."

Lily peered through the ICU window at Angela. Still on the ventilator with tubes in her nose. A nurse in scrubs was taking notes from a monitor.

"Can she hear?" Lily asked.

"She's in a coma."

"What's with her hands?" They were lashed to the bedrails.

"To protect her." The charge nurse signaled the one in scrubs to close the blinds. "She tried to pull the tubes out."

Bully for Angela! "When will she wake up?"

"You'll have to talk to the doctor—"

"I'm her medical POA. Lily Sparks."

The charge nurse looked at Angela's chart. "Cousin?"

"Why?" Lily asked.

"You're listed as next of kin. Like I told her lawyer—"

"Lawyer?" Pinstriped buzzards.

"I told him and that jowly cop—"

Johnson.

"—just missed him," the nurse said. "He came back for her clothes."

Rockies, her ass. "Did he take everything?" Lily asked.

"I'll check."

The charge nurse went into the ICU. She returned with a large white plastic bag.

"We have her purse and shoes."

All Lily could see was that red SUV. Which shoes had Angela been wearing? She reached for the bag.

The nurse held on. "I can't give this to you."

"Just a look," Lily begged.

"Ms. Sparks, it's 2:00 a.m."

"I'm her cousin, for God's sake!"

"Don't make me call a guard." Her expression softened; the ICU must bring out the worst in visitors. "Go home, dear. Get some sleep."

Chapter Twenty-Seven

When Lily pulled up at the airport Sunday afternoon, Sasha was curbside in a trim navy pantsuit, a leather purse twice her size and a matching overnight bag. She offered her cheek, and Lily pecked it before stowing her bags in the Prius's backseat.

Sasha looked up at the open blue sky.

"Heavens!" she exclaimed. "Hopper and Jo traveled the West in their '54 Buick, but your airport's in the middle of nowhere. I never thought I'd be back so soon."

"Thanks for coming," Lily said. "You're the only one I could call."

"Don't be absurd." Sasha was suddenly all business. "When's the next flash mob?"

"Wednesday."

"Damn that symposium!" She had to be back at Yale on Tuesday. "Do we know which Hopper it is?"

"Nobody's returned my texts. Where do we start?"

"Take me to Angela."

Lily pulled out of the airport and headed for I-70. As they drove from the sere plains to Denver's industrial outskirts, she told Sasha about the gloves at The Oxford.

"Hotel lobbies are social petri dishes," Sasha said. "A guest or movers could've left them. And maybe it isn't what gloves meant to Hopper, but what they mean to the killer. Or what he thinks they meant."

Lily thought of Elizabeth Griffiths Smith's arthritic fingers. "Maybe it's about hands."

Sasha frowned. "Hands?"

"Maybe he made Vanessa cover hers because they tempted him, or—"

"What?"

"—to preserve the illusion that she was ageless."

"Hah!" Sasha looked ruefully at her own wrinkled hands. "A message about hypocrisy, a latter-day Dorian Gray?" Seeing Lily's baffled look, she shook her head in despair. "Don't tell me you never read Oscar Wilde's tale of the haunted portrait! It aged while its handsome subject remained youthful. But let's not take this life-imitating-art bit too far."

Denver's skyline glinted in the afternoon sun.

"But Vanessa was old enough to be a character actress," Lily insisted. "Maybe he was rebuking her for thinking she could pull off a striptease."

"Or the gloves are simply a fetish." Sasha shuddered. "God knows what turns on men like him. Don't forget the fuck-me's."

—

The ICU was bustling, and Gina's bouquet needed water. Luckily there was a different charge nurse.

"I'm Ms. Kurtz's POA and next of kin," Lily told her. "Can we see her?"

"Sorry, miss." The nurse glanced longingly at the group in the office comparing notes for a shift change. "Ms. Kurtz is in no condition for visitors."

Sasha gave her a gimlet look. "I've come two thousand miles to see her."

"Sorry, ma'am."

That did it.

Sasha squared her shoulders. "I am Angela's teacher and oldest friend!"

Before the nurse could do anything, Sasha marched into the ICU. Lily followed her in. Shaking off a nurse in scrubs, Sasha went straight to Angela's bed. The scrub nurse moved in, but a fierce look from Sasha drove her back. Sasha leaned over Angela and whispered in her ear. Angela stirred and the nurse gasped. She turned and waved to the charge nurse. Lily quickly looked around.

The plastic bag with Angela's purse and shoes was on the floor by her bed. The cord cinching it had come loose, and she saw a flash of blue. She nudged Sasha and pointed to the bag. Sasha rose from Angela's side. Her eyes widened.

"The shoes," she hissed. "Grab 'em!"

The charge nurse was coming with reinforcements. Kneeling, Lily thrust Angela's sandals into Sasha's purse and snapped it shut. She rose and faced the nurse. "Sorry, no harm meant."

"Leave now!"

———

In the parking lot they opened Sasha's purse. Size 10 stilettos. Those ridiculous shoes, Cam called them. One toe was scuffed and the sole torn, but both straps were intact. Angela didn't trip. And it was no accident.

Like Vanessa's fuck-me's, her stilettos were peacock blue.

Chapter Twenty-Eight

Sun batters the windows, steam and chlorine make the air sweat. The water is fuck-me blue. At the end of the lane the lone swimmer executes a flip.

"We have a master class," the girl in the tracksuit says. She has pretty hands. "Little brush-up on technique, perhaps some yoga?"

"I competed in college," you tell her.

"Awesome!" She giggles. Not brays like Angela.

"Blew my cuff doing fly." You rotate your shoulder gingerly. "Put on a couple pounds since then."

"We have just the trainer for you! Darcie—"

The clock at the end of the pool glows red, its digits flash white. Seconds sliced to tenths. In black googles and a bathing cap, the swimmer is a cyborg. Well-built. Hung. Smooth-muscled machine in Lycra trunks, slave to that Orwellian clock. Back and forth. Times himself, doesn't need to look. Sixty-second fly, backstroke every ten laps. Punishing, masochistic. Not getting laid, Paul?

"Saltwater?" you ask.

"Of course!" Tracksuit rattles off trivia about the pool.

Paul turns onto his back. The scar is a shiny cord, a raised furrow slicing through graying curls from abdomen to pecs. For some women it's a turn-on. A different kind of sword fight.

"…kale smoothies at the snack bar…" In her track shoes, Tracksuit shifts like a skittish colt. You picture her in open-toe stilettos. "We offer packages. Perhaps—"

"I'm interested in a corporate membership."

"Awesome." She squints. "How many employees?"

"Twenty-five." You laugh modestly. "Ex-jocks, engineers. I'm sure Darcie—"

"—or Devin!" She wrinkles her nose.

"—can whip us into shape. We're doing a triathlon. That's why I'm interested in the pool."

She exhales. "Gotcha."

Paul winds down with an extra lap of backstroke. Under the fluorescent light the scar gleams like raw liver. Poor bastard. What was his excuse for showing up on her doorstep, a fancy new job? Under different circumstances—vastly different—they might even have been friends.

"Too bad the office is closed," you tell Tracksuit. It's Sunday and the cubicle in the lobby is dark. When Paul takes off his goggles the light will blind him just long enough. What'll it be then—a six-minute shower, ice cold?

"Give me your card," she says, but doesn't reach for it. "Devin will call you."

Not Darcie. "I'll leave it at the desk. Can I hang around, grab a smoothie?"

"Awesome!" Tracksuit can't wait to get away.

—

The concrete stairwell's drafty, a good ten degrees colder than the pool deck. On Paul's smooth shoulders beads of water jiggle. You can take him at the landing, or in the shower. Cut him all the way down. A couple of guys in ratty T-shirts and smelly shorts push past you to the locker room. But Paul's a creature of habit. There will be another time.

—

Paul enters the lobby. Gym bag, sneakers, Levi's. Wet hair.

You follow him to his rental car in the building's garage. Paul drives past The Westin and up Seventeenth. Anticipating him turning south to her place, from three cars behind you signal right. But he goes past the turn to Cheesman Park. He turns left.

Did you have this wrong?

Paul parks.

You pass Paul. He doesn't notice.

What the fuck?

He's watching a townhouse at The East.

Chapter Twenty-Nine

Over breakfast early Monday at a diner, Lily and Sasha mapped out their plan.

"Fuck-me's and a pair of gloves aren't enough," Sasha declared, "nor the slaying of Vanessa and the attempt on Angela's life. To read the killer's next move, we must get into his head."

Too wired after yesterday's escapade at the ICU to eat, Lily sipped coffee. She'd invited Sasha to stay at her condo, but she'd insisted room service at midnight was one of the pleasures of travel. "If he identifies with Hopper—"

"—the answer's in the paintings." Sasha speared her bacon with a vengeance. "More precisely, one."

"We need the pattern," Lily agreed. "But how do we know there is one, or that the right painting's in the show? *Girlie Show* isn't."

Sasha waved her fork dismissively. "Every artist tells a story, Lily— like writers, the same one over and over. Trust me, your Hoppers tell the story the killer reads to himself at night."

"So where do we start?"

Sasha stabbed the last piece of bacon. "We'll focus on Hopper's women."

—

An hour before the museum opened, Lily badged them in at the loading dock.

The exhibition gallery was eerily quiet, and they did a quick walk-though. Lily knew all the paintings but had never seen them hanging together. In the mauve room, a display case of Jo's spiralbound diaries blocked traffic; they detoured around it, scanning the walls. What had seemed too few paintings were suddenly too many.

"Let's go back to the beginning," Sasha suggested.

They retraced their steps to the entrance. Just past the *Nighthawks* screen, the exhibition proper opened with an oil of a woman in a red dress sitting on a bed in front of a picture window. Behind it, Hopper had painted the front end of a large green car with a sleek chrome ornament on its hood. "*Western Motel*, 1957." Sasha chuckled fondly. "How they fought over that damn Buick! Hopper was a lousy driver, but he refused to let Jo take the wheel."

The first room's dove-gray walls were hung with New England landscapes featuring lighthouses. "Phallic," Sasha murmured. The periwinkle room had a rural storefront and a row of deserted looking redbrick buildings on a city block. She gestured to the fire hydrant and barber pole. "I rest my case."

"The women," Lily reminded her.

In the next room, mauve walls framed the cinema usherette, a buxom secretary in a tight dress at a filing cabinet, and an elderly woman in furs gazing out a lobby window. Those were followed by a painting of a spooky Victorian mansion behind some railroad tracks. Then came a painting of a slender bobbed-hair girl who perched at the edge of a bed in a boyish chemise. A cloche was on the dresser and a valise and suitcase stood by a chair.

"*Hotel Room*, 1931," Sasha said wistfully. "The modern age."

Lily examined the painting more closely. The girl was gazing at some kind of folded paper in her lap. It was too big for a romance novel and too small for a period magazine, but she was absorbed in it.

The last painting was *Couple near Poplars*. Sasha tsk-tsked. "Poor Hopper! What happened in Paris didn't stay there. Some historians believe the girl was Alta."

Lily scanned the mauve walls, skipping from one painting to the next. Gibson Girl, Beret Man—the girl with the paper in her lap. They all ran together, but nothing fit.

In the sage room was a painting of a bald man in a shirt with gartered sleeves slumped on a curb smoking a cigar. Then came *Room in New York's* married couple with the newspaper and piano. Next a wooded road at twilight with a man in a silk vest and tie at a Mobil station pumping gas, followed by *Summer Evening's* front porch. Each painting was competently hung and spaced, but they were starting to spin.

"I told you to eat, dear," Sasha said. "Is the cafeteria open?"

"It's the paintings. They're a hopeless jumble."

"You didn't expect them to be chronologically displayed," Sasha sniffed. "Not even Gina's as unimaginative as that. Maybe she hung them by wall color."

Lily shook her head. Color-sorting pieces was the first step to solving a jigsaw puzzle, but… "What's missing is the picture, Sasha. There's no story, no arc!"

"Then rearrange them, Lily—"

Voices and metal squeaking on wood interrupted them. The museum opened in twenty minutes, and back in the mauve room, Kip and James were moving the display case. They looked up at Lily and Sasha in surprise, and the dolly almost slipped. "Jeez!" Kip said.

"Didn't mean to scare you," Lily said. "Cook's tour."

James saluted. "Nice to see you, prof."

Sasha wagged her finger playfully. "Just making sure you do Hopper justice."

"If Gina lets us," he said with a grin. Behind him, the girl in *Hotel Room* was studying the paper in her lap.

"A monologue," Lily said softly. "What's in her lap, Sasha?"

"Jo's diary said a train schedule."

"What?" Kip said.

Lily turned back to them. "Gina will pitch a fit if you don't move that case!" She took Sasha's arm and drew her aside. "We've been looking at this all wrong," she said urgently. "I've been trying to track where the woman goes next by her age in the paintings. But she's eternal—ageless— so the arc is her relationship with the man. That's the killer's flashpoint."

Sasha furrowed her brow, then slowly nodded.

"Start with *Automat*," Lily said. "Girl—"

"—alone in a diner, contemplating her fate."

"Then *Summer Evening*—"

Sasha nodded vigorously. "Girl and boy on porch, him pleading to get to first base."

"Now *Room in New York…*"

"… married couple ignoring each other. And in *Hotel Room…*"

"…she's on the move." Wednesday's Hopper. "It's about her leaving him, Sasha."

Lily went back to Kip. "Who decides which Hoppers get staged?"

He shrugged. "Consensus, I guess. Me and Gina and the folks at Offbeat."

"Where will the next one be?" If she knew the location, Paul could get Johnson to stake it out.

Kip and James exchanged an uneasy glance. "You know we can't—"

"Sasha!" Gina cried. "What a surprise!" She was with an entourage of docents. "You're in Denver for my tour?"

"To see Angela."

Gina made a sad face. "Perhaps lunch. I'll call Michel."

"Cancel Wednesday's show," Lily said. "And the gala."

Gina looked suspiciously at Kip and James.

"They've got nothing to do with this," Lily said.

"Are you out of your frigging—" Gina began. She turned and grimaced at the docents. "Our Conservator of Paintings is having her usual fun."

If *Hotel Room* was the last micro-drama, which hotel would it be?

She looked at James and Kip again. No help there.

Only one place to turn.

Chapter Thirty

Lily dropped Sasha at the airport. Paul's phone went to voice mail and he wasn't returning texts. That litigation firm must be wining and dining him. Suddenly the weight of the last two days descended. This was no game. If she hadn't taken her eye off the ball, Angela wouldn't be fighting for her life, and if she was right about *Hotel Room*, Rachel could be next. To stop the killer, she needed Paul. Drive to The Westin and surprise him? Or get some sleep. She had one more day to figure out where the drama would be staged.

She texted Ernie. *U free?*

Offbeat, he replied.

—

Again, the theater was deserted.

"Ernie?" she called.

Laird Bennett emerged from the box office.

She hadn't seen him since the night Vanessa was killed. He'd been in the balcony for the striptease but wasn't at the party in the lobby later. He came closer, and she smelled something rank.

"You're the one who found Vee," he said.

A lifetime ago. "How awful for your troupe."

"Rachel's more than ready to step in." Lily tried to breathe without inhaling. "How long before you knew Vee was dead?"

"Mr. Bennett—"

"—Laird. I feel we're on a first-name basis."

"Why?" His shaggy mane and disproportionately large head belonged on a forest animal. A Picasso-like satyr who lived on wild garlic, bad wine and small furry creatures. Lily took another step back.

He shook his head in amusement. "You're not much of an actress."

"I'm a paintings conservator."

"You're here because of Vee."

"Mr. Bennett—"

"—Laird." His halitosis was overpowering. Was he using it to intimidate her?

"I'm a conservator, not a detective."

He snorted. "Who noses around the Kennedy Center."

For that to have gotten back to Laird, Paul must have gone beyond the sealed file. "Do you have something to hide?"

"You should be looking at Andy Bragg," he said, "or Cam."

"I'm looking for Ernie," Lily said.

"That pipsqueak?" He laughed nastily.

So the thing between him and the fussy stage manager was mutual. "He did a damn good job designing your sets."

"*Sweeney Todd?*" Laird shrugged. "Vee was just enough over the hill for Mrs. Lovett, but Ernie's lights did shine off the central prop."

"And *Rope?*"

"I wanted to update Leopold and Loeb—rich boys gone bad in our own Gilded Age."

This was a waste of time. Lily checked her phone. Nothing from Paul.

"Your FBI agent?" Laird smirked. "I've still got friends at the Kennedy Center, by the way."

"Where's Ernie?" she demanded.

"Backstage. Say hi to the FBI from me."

In the pitch-dark auditorium, Lily felt her way down to the stage. Behind the break in the curtain on the back wall was the door. Backstage was dimly lit. Wasn't there a central corridor, with workshops and dressing rooms branching off? Voices...

"Ernie?" she called.

Something echoed back. Like at the exhibition gallery, the partitions stopped short of the ceiling. The further she went, the farther the voices seemed, and a swamp cooler or generator distorted the sound. Backstage was a Turkish souk, and she was in too deep to see an Exit sign.

The swamp cooler abruptly shut off. Warm air descended like a blanket, and now exhaustion really hit. For forty-eight hours she'd been running on coffee and Sasha's fumes.

Go back to the beginning and ask Laird.

She turned and hit a partition.

She giggled nervously.

Lights flickered.

"Ernie?"

They'd forgotten she was here, or thought she'd left. If anyone but Laird knew she was here at all. This was a rat trap—a violation of every provision in the fire code. She stopped and took a breath. The carpentry shop was to the left, wasn't it? Did that mean the dressing rooms were on the right? Find the central corridor. She went twenty paces back to what could be the main path and turned right. This was the gallery all over again: trying to summon order where everything was askew. She still wasn't seeing the whole story, but it didn't end at *Hotel Room*. The grand finale would be the gala.

She came to three unmarked doors.

The first was locked.

The second room had a blackboard and a stack of folding chairs.

The third opened onto a tufted green velvet sofa, a floor lamp with frosted glass, and a side table with a silver ice bucket and crystal decanter.

What was a shrine to the Roaring Twenties doing here? In the corner was a steamer trunk. On top sat a coil of rope.

Of course! This must be Ernie's set for *Rope*, the take-off on the nihilistic murder of a Chicago boy. She opened the trunk, half-expecting to find a body inside. Instead it was filled with flyers and programs for the play, and a folded life-sized carboard cutout of two smirking college kids with slicked-back hair and slim-fit suits. Was that Bo in the round spectacles, or was he the one holding the rope?

The lights went out.

Shit.

She tried to find the wall but hit the couch. This was ridiculous. Her phone had a flashlight. She dug though her purse. Her screen lit long enough to announce the battery was dead. She felt along the wall until she reached the door. The corridor was black. From somewhere to her left came footsteps.

"Laird?"

This is what she got for butting into his pathetic past. He was messing with her, punishing her for the Kennedy Center and Paul. He'd jump out and… The footsteps stopped.

She heard breathing. His—or hers? In the darkness she was completely alone.

Make the footsteps happen again.

Enough.

She was here to stop the next show.

"Ernie?"

He'd give her his charger and she'd call Paul.

Footsteps resumed. Softer, lighter—almost a scurrying.

"Rachel?"

Paul would call Johnson.

"Bo?"

The footsteps were heavier. Closer. She was being herded to the right.

If this was all her frigging imagination and Andy Bragg was the killer, she and Paul would laugh about it with their grandkids.

She smacked into a wall. It opened and lights flashed in her face.

A man with a bloody smock and a mad grin came straight at her.

Chapter Thirty-One

"Lily?"

Ernie.

"I—" She couldn't speak.

"Hey, you okay?" He moved in for a hug but stopped. "Laird told me you were here. I see you met our Mad Barber of Fleet Street."

Leaning forward with his elbow raised at throat level, the wax effigy seemed poised to spring. His hands were empty but his face was grotesquely lifelike—simultaneously crazed, sullen and amused.

"He won't hurt you," Ernie assured her. "And don't let the set scare you."

The bright overhead light caromed from Sweeney's sweaty brow to an antique reclining chair to a steel table. The set was a cross between Fritz Lang's futuristic industrial plant, a midwestern slaughterhouse, and an insane dental office.

"The sponsors loved the staging so much they sprang for a Madame Tussaud's." Ernie peered at Sweeney and frowned. "I told Laird to stop those tours."

"Tours?"

"Schoolkids can't get enough of Sweeney, and sometimes they take a souvenir. I hate people messing with my props." Sweeney's razor was missing. Ernie looked at Lily. "What? You don't think the killer—"

"Of course not." Laird had been fucking with her. Was Ernie doing that too?

He laughed. "Sometimes a razor's just a razor."

The killer liked props. But Ernie was a stickler for accuracy, he knew art was in the details. Cam had said he'd wanted Vanessa to wear just one glove, not two. And if he had anything to hide he wouldn't have opened the theater to her. With lights on, things began to look familiar. They passed the carpentry shop. Rachel's dressing room was to the left. "Gone for the night," Ernie said. "Tomorrow's a big day. She's rehearsing for Wednesday, then a real play. Cam wrote it, it's her big break-out."

They took the stage door to the auditorium. Lily stumbled on the steps up the aisle.

"Poor thing, you're beat," Ernie said. "Working on the gala?"

"Gina's department."

"I dropped by the lab and saw Matt. What's gotten into him, anyway? He looks awfully chipper. Did he finally ask that pretty girl out?"

"What?" She was still trying to wrap her head around Sweeney's missing razor.

"Your colleague's assistant."

Willow? The museum was a hive of gossip. "We need to cancel Wednesday's show, Ernie."

"But Rachel's been rehearsing all week!"

Hotel Room. Would her monologue be a paean to Hopper's newly modern world where the trains ran on time, or an ode to slipping the leash? There was one more day. Paul was tied up in interviews, but tomorrow night they were taking Dad to dinner. She'd make her case to Paul, and he'd tell Johnson. "Which hotel will it be, Ernie?"

He didn't bother denying it. "We're looking at a few places," he said cagily. "Cam, Laird, Gina, Kip… they find out we're talking, my head's on the block."

"If you care about Rachel—"

"She'll be safe," he insisted.

"Bo won't be there."

"But I will! I can protect her."

Lily shook her head. "We can't take any chances."

"Gina's texting me Wednesday morning. I'll tell you the minute I know."

Chapter Thirty-Two

Tuesday flew by with last-minute inspections of the paintings on-site. At 4:30 p.m. Paul picked her up in his rental car. She'd made reservations at the Italian place in Cherry Creek where she'd gone with Dad to celebrate her conservation degree.

"How was the game?" she asked Paul.

"Saturday night?" Paul said. Sasha's whirlwind visit made it seem a lifetime ago. "You know Johnson—beer and brats."

"What was the score?"

Paul laughed. "Hell, Lily—it's the Rockies!"

"You saw both games?" On Saturday night, the ICU nurse had said she'd barely missed running into Johnson.

"What is this," Paul said lightly, "I need season Broncos tickets too?"

"I bet Johnson likes football."

"Football? We're talking Broncos, Lily." He pulled into the lot at Dad's building and parked. "Speaking of sleuthing, you know that Kennedy Center thing? Laird Bennett does have a history. What's interesting is the women he harassed. Character actresses."

Surprise, surprise. She'd been planning to wait until after dinner, but the time was now. "You have to get Johnson to pull the plug."

"On what?"

"Hopper. Tomorrow's flash mob, the gala—the works."

"But Andy Bragg—"

"Don't bullshit me, Paul! Vanessa's murder was no one-off. He was at The Oxford, and then Angela was pushed." Dad came out of the big glass doors and looked for her Prius. Not seeing it, he sat on a bench. He could wait for once. Paul already knew about Hoppin' Mad's missives to Sasha and Gina. Now Lily told him about *Girlie Show*, The Oxford's gloves, Angela's peacock fuck-me's, and Hopper's woman's arc. He stared out the windshield and waited until she ran out of breath.

"Go back to Vanessa's murder, Lily. Connect the dots."

"He dressed her before he slit her throat, Paul. He made her put on gloves and jammed her feet in those fuck-me's."

"Why?"

"He was trying to humiliate her, Paul, put her in her place. Punish her for her vanity or sexual power. If he identifies with Hopper, maybe he's trying to get even for some woman in Hopper's past."

"But Hopper didn't kill anyone." Paul popped the key from the ignition and reached for the door.

She grabbed his arm. "He's going past where Hopper stopped."

"You and Sasha and a bunch of art theory—"

"It's not just about *Girlie Show*, or even Vanessa." She slowed down to make every word count. "He's taken Hopper into real time with Gina and Sasha and Angela, and he's saying he's not done." Dad had risen and was scanning the parking lot. "Look, Paul. Maybe it's not Laird Bennett. But he's into staging and props, and he'll be at *Hotel Room* tomorrow."

"Why *Hotel Room*?"

"It's the next chapter, and Cam said—"

"Cam Maddox?" He turned and frowned. "What the hell were you—"

Dad was coming down the walk. Paul opened the door and strode to meet him with hand outstretched. "Sorry to keep you waiting, Mr.

Sparks. I'm looking forward to getting acquainted."

"When one of us isn't about to be killed?" Dad said irritably.

Paul grinned. "That too. Catch the double-header the other night?"

"What does an FBI man know about baseball?"

Paul shrugged. "I'm from Iowa."

—

Paul ordered a bottle of Malbec. She'd told him Dad didn't drink.

"You liked the lasagna last time, Dad, remember?"

He left his wine untouched. "I have something else to thank you for, Mr. Reilly." Besides saving his life? She squeezed Paul's hand. "My daughter leaving the practice of law, where she was about to make partner."

Paul sipped his Malbec. "Marvelous, isn't it, to raise a daughter with the guts to leave something she's good at for something she actually cares about?"

"Guts?" He snorted. "You call art—"

"Dad."

A white-haired foursome in pastel sweaters glanced over. Early dinner after a game of golf. The woman in the green sweater paused over her tiramisu and smiled at Lily sympathetically.

The waiter returned and they ordered pasta.

"Paul, tell us about that litigation firm," Lily said.

"I'd rather talk about what you're up to." He turned to Dad. "Hopper puts Lily on the map, Mr. Sparks. She can write her own ticket—"

Like the girl with the train schedule.

"—and go wherever she wants."

"Go?" Dad cried.

"You should be very proud—"

"She doesn't want to leave!"

The golfers looked over again. Nothing like a little dinner theater. Who'd be the first to pull out a smart-phone and start recording? The man in pink nodded knowingly at Paul.

The waiter hustled over with a platter of antipasto they hadn't ordered. He murmured *on the house* to Lily and topped off her Malbec. She took an artichoke heart. Dad lifted his fork, then stopped. He fixed Paul with his beadiest glare.

"I know what this is about, Mr. Reilly." He was seething. "Think you can buy me with red sauce and Malbec?"

The golfers had abandoned their dessert. The entire bar was watching.

Paul set down his fork. "I love Lily, Mr. Sparks, and you can't do a damn thing about it."

"You—"

"But out of curiosity, what's your price?"

"More than an FBI—"

Paul opened his billfold and showed it to him. The restaurant fell silent.

Lily rose and dialed for a Lyft.

"Where are you going?" Paul said.

"As far as I can get!" To hell with the audience. "Why won't I commit to you? Just look across the table!"

Chapter Thirty-Three

The Thin Man aims for hipsters and the Russian mob but misses. Noir wars with Christmas lights, crucifixes, and house-infused dill-pickle vodka. The snacks barely meet a tavern's minimum requirement for food. There's nothing happy about this happy hour.

The East is around the corner. Transient singles, rootless and footloose. Degrees without job security. Lawyers doing contract work at fancy downtown firms, medical personnel roaming between urgent care centers on the Front Range and the Western Slope. Looking for some action to take the edge off? The Thin Man ain't your place. Which makes your quarry a mystery.

You watch Nick Lang—his name is on The East's directory—on the barstool drinking vodka. Nick has all the latest gadgets. Bluetooth wireless earbuds, the all-black military men's outdoor sports watch, the slimmest smartphone. He dresses the part, too. Black T-shirt, aviator shades, straight jeans tight but not too tight. His wavy auburn hair is slicked back and tapered at the sides. On Nick, even the busted nose looks good.

Nick tosses off another double vodka. Seriously drinking, not cruising the off-duty nurses and actresses between parts. He taps his hand on his knee, swings the steel tip of his boot against the bar. The barkeep is generous with the pour. Nick checks his watch like he's expecting someone. Does he know he's being followed? Or is he waiting for somebody?

Take that chubby blonde in scrubs two tables over. An ER nurse? Blondie's been eyeing Nick all night. She leaves her pals and detours to the bar to brush by Nick. He hunches over his drink. She gives up on him and heads your way. You smile but not too wide. *Buy you a drink, dear?* As she goes past you towards the john, you bend like you're picking something off the floor.

"Oh, miss?" you call out.

Blondie turns.

"You dropped this." You show her a twenty-dollar bill—if only it were a glove! A variation on the gambit the other night with Ponytail and the cocktail napkin, though the drama's tamer without Prettyboy watching from behind the bar. You're warming up for a double-header. Not just tomorrow's show—*how dare she toy with me, after what I've done for her!*—but the new turf you're cutting with Nick tonight. Not just a new script, a new type of prey. For that you must be limber.

"Don't think so," Blondie says. Her purse is closed, and her scrubs don't have pockets.

"It was stuck to your shoe." Ugly sneakers. Not your type.

"Thanks, but—"

Her friends are watching. You hold the twenty out to her. "Take it." You know you want to. "You've earned it."

Blondie tosses her hair. Are you some sicko creep pimping her, or genuinely nice? It's a public place, she has the upper hand. The floor's wet and the twenty could've stuck to her shoe. Who knows, maybe it even did fall from her purse.

What's her price?

A twenty buys a lipstick, a cheap but pretty one. Whatever she decides, her friends will have her back. She takes the money and continues to the john. She'll think about it later tonight in bed. She'll say to herself, *What did he mean, I earned it?*

At the bar, Nick's on his third double vodka. He has forced you to rethink. Lily's more challenging than Ponytail or Vanessa or Blondie. Fuck, she'll *have* to love you. But it's been one shitty thing after the other. First Angela—that laugh, Jesus, you thought you'd never get it out of your head! Then Paul, showing up out of nowhere. Now Nick.

Why is Paul following Nick? And what's Nick doing in Denver?

Nick is a cipher. Sold his house six months ago and dropped off the grid. No social media networks or sites. No next of kin, not even a dog. Cocky smoothness around gadgets and machines, some kind of engineer, all of a sudden turns up in Denver at The East. He's planning something, and Paul's on to him. Which means he has something Paul wants.

Her.

So what if Paul's with her tonight? He won't score. Nick's got the confidence—the arrogance—to land her. Paul never will. You'll be watching when he leaves in the morning. An antiseptic kiss is what he'll get. That scar on his chest makes him defective. A loser, and he knows it. Probably can't get it up. Which makes Nick the real threat.

Nick rises and drops a fistful of bills on the bar.

You can do this.

With a cheery wave to Blondie, you follow Nick from the bar. He goes down the block and around the corner to The East. Staggering slightly—one double vodka too many. No sign of Paul. At the door to his townhouse, Nick fumbles with the key fob and drops it.

You pick it up for him.

Nick looks up in surprise. "Thanks, man."

Nick opens the door.

Do it.

You shove Nick inside and bolt the door.

"What the fuck?" Nick says.

Chapter Thirty-Four

Outside her condo door, Paul was waiting.

"Where the hell have you been?" he demanded.

Racking up a fortune on a Lyft. The driver should have tipped her for listening to him pour his heart out over elementary school teaching not paying the rent, and not being able to get second dates with girls he met at bars. He wasn't bad looking, it was his neediness. There seemed to be a lot of that going around.

"Not tonight, Paul." She unlocked the door. "I'm really tired."

"You walked out and left me with your father."

"I'm too tired to fight." She went to the kitchen and gave Jack some kibble. Paul was right behind her.

"Not half as tired as I am with this bullshit. You at least owe me a drink."

She put the kibble away and poured them whiskey. Paul set his on the counter and loosened his tie. The gray in his hair had distracted her from the deep circles under his eyes. "Did you take Dad home?"

"No."

"You left him?"

"After a real meal."

"You stayed?"

"With half the bar taking bets on the first punch? We went to a burger joint."

"Dad hates—"

"You don't know the first thing about him, Lily." Paul undid his collar. He was wearing his black pinstriped suit. Another interview, or was he trying to impress Dad? She'd been so busy trying to convince him to have Johnson cancel *Hotel Room* tomorrow she hadn't even noticed. She took their drinks and sat with him on the couch.

"Why did you leave the FBI?" she asked.

"Following a lead."

"What lead?"

"Tell you when it's over." He untied his shoes and laid his head back. She settled in next to him and he slipped his arm around her. She'd almost forgotten how good he smelled. Not his aftershave, but— "You made a pretty good case for *Hotel Room* earlier."

"Now you can make it to Johnson," she said. "Tell him to shut it down."

Paul sipped his whiskey. "Because someone left gloves on a piano and Angela and Vanessa wore blue fuck-me's? He'll need more."

She set down her drink. "At least stake it out."

"Where?"

"Ernie's texting me."

"The rabbit?" He laughed wearily. "If you stay away from Cam Maddox…"

She locked her little finger in his. "Pinky swear."

"Geez, does this mean we're going steady?" He nuzzled her neck and she slid her hand to his thigh. "Or are you trying to take advantage of me?"

"Stay and I just might."

Paul pulled her onto his lap. They kissed long and slow. "Poor old Johnson," he murmured. "He'll never know how he was bribed."

"Bribed?"

"To shut down an art show."

He stroked her hair, and she laid her head on his chest. His heart was strong and steady, his scar coiled and tensed to the beat. They'd wasted enough time. When this was over, there'd be decisions to make. How she wanted it to be over! "When Ernie texts, you'll call Johnson?"

Paul's hand paused. "If you'll leave it to him."

She sat up. "And not go?"

"Don't you have a Gentileschi to clean," he tried, "or a condition report to write?"

"I owe it to—"

"—Angela?" Paul shook his head. "Too big a risk."

"For the killer, not me. And Johnson will be there."

"Lily—"

"I'm going, Paul."

She went to the kitchen for refills.

"You're staying tonight?" she said over her shoulder.

No answer.

He and Jack were snoring on the couch.

Chapter Thirty-Five

Paul had a whopping ticket from parking overnight at her condo. He walked her to her Prius. "You're not going alone tonight. The minute Ernie texts, call me."

"What about your lead?" Lily asked.

"Lead?" He seemed confused. "Oh, that. Never mind."

"You look like you slept in your suit." He did, on her couch. "What about your interviews?"

"They're doing the full-court press, an all-day dog-and-pony show for clients." His arm tightened around her, but he still wouldn't name the firm. "I need to shower and change, grab a swim. The minute you hear—"

"Promise." She gave him a quick kiss, then couldn't help leaning in for more before letting him go. His hunger made her want more.

—

Michel called a last-minute meeting for the admin staff and gala crew. Gina announced that Angela's condition was unchanged. She was still wrangling with Kip and James over display cases. Nobody mentioned Vanessa's murder or this evening's micro-drama. On the way out, Lily grabbed Ernie.

"News?" she asked.

"On what?"

"The hotel!"

"Down to three," he whispered. Gina was headed their way. He waved to her and she froze. Friendliness always confused her. "Brown Palace, Teatro—"

"Not good enough."

"For whom?" Ernie said.

Lily stopped herself from blowing Johnson's stakeout just in time.

"Rachel has the monologue down pat," he continued. "It's hysterical, even without the improv. The crowd will love it."

"We need to warn her," Lily said, "and have Bo standing by."

He shook his head. "He's in rehearsals. Laird will pitch a fit…"

"Screw Laird!"

Ernie sobered up. "Okay, I'll make sure Bo and Kip are there. We want that bastard as much as you do."

—

Ernie's text came at 5:40 p.m. *Brown Palace.*

The wedge-shaped sandstone landmark was on the other side of Civic Center Park. Lily texted Paul to meet her there and got a Lyft.

In The Brown Palace's atrium, waiters in black uniforms were cleaning up after high tea. She and Paul gazed up at eight rows of balconies crowned by a stained-glass skylight.

Paul suppressed a yawn. "Could be anywhere."

"No—a guest room."

"There's two hundred and fifty."

Two guys in sport coats were chatting up the female piano player.

"Johnson's men," Paul explained.

"They're doing a lot of good!"

"Relax. A cubbyhole in a theater is one thing, but this is The Brown Palace. The killer would be nuts to try anything here." Paul conferred with the plainclothes officers, who summoned the general manager. The men huddled and shrugged.

"You sure it was The Brown Palace?" Paul asked her.

She texted Ernie. *Where R U?*

A moment later he pinged.

Teatro! Last minute!

Other end of LoDo. Lily and Paul grabbed a cab.

Chapter Thirty-Six

The Teatro was an upscale boutique hotel with a stylish black awning and white terracotta trim. Paul squeezed her knee. "This is more like it," he said. "I can see a killer striking here, and there's half as many rooms. If he doesn't, maybe we can book—"

"Call Johnson."

"By the time his guys get here, it'll be over. Including the flash mob, if one even materializes." He rang the bell at the desk. The clerk was drinking espresso at the coffee bar. He sauntered over.

"We're here for an event," Paul said.

"The Center for Performing Arts is just down—"

"We're with the museum," Lily said. "They're staging a show."

"Oh, yes! A girl just—"

"Where?" Paul asked.

"Sixth floor."

They rode the elevator up. At the end of the hallway a door was ajar. Lily pushed it open.

The guest room had an antique chest of drawers, a stuffed armchair, and a single bed. Rachel sat at the edge. Hair and costume had transformed her into yet another Hopper girl: one whose bronze bob was softened by a marcel wave, and whose pink chemise and flowered silk kimono accentuated her sloping shoulders and boyish build. She gazed down at the train schedule.

"Rachel?" Lily said.

As in the painting, old-fashioned pumps with diagonal straps and an ornate buckle lay on the rug as if she'd just kicked them off. A green cloche sat on the bureau, and an unopened valise and suitcase stood on the floor. Unlike in Hopper's day, the room was air-conditioned. There was no sign of Bo or Kip, and Rachel's fingers curled around something.

"Rachel?" Lily said again. Paul gripped her shoulder to stop her from going in.

Footsteps and a whistle came down the hall. Ernie with a bounce in his step and James with a tray of iced lattes.

"Glad you made it, guys!" Ernie said. "Laird nixed The Brown because the rooms were too big. Luckily we'd scouted The Teatro." He gave Lily and Paul lattes and thick black straws from James's tray. "Rachel's been rehearsing all day. Figured she could use it."

Paul set the lattes and straws on the table outside the door.

"Where's Laird?" Ernie asked. "He promised to stay till we got back. There was no barista in the lobby so we went to Starbucks." He peeked through the door. "Isn't she perfect? We got that old schedule from Union Station…."

Paul stepped between him and Lily, blocking the view.

Ernie frowned and took the tray from James. He looked past Paul. "That armchair should be closer to the closet. And why's Rachel wearing the kimono? It should be on the chair. Rach, are you cold?"

"What's in her hand?" James asked.

Chin to her chest, Rachel continued to stare down. Ernie started to move forward but Paul blocked the doorway. "Who else was here?" he asked as he calmly punched a number in his phone.

"Bo's supposed…" Ernie elbowed past Paul, jiggling the lattes in the tray. "Rach? I got you a blonde vanilla grande—"

Something unnatural in the angle of her head.

"Lily—" She fiercely shook Paul off and went in.

Lily touched Rachel and the kimono fell away. Her shoulders were mottled, and her neck had purple grooves. Her eyes bulged. Pink froth and a bloody tongue protruded from her gaping mouth.

Ernie dropped the tray and screamed. "Rachel!"

Hopper's girl hadn't slipped the leash.

Her head was lashed to her body by piano wire.

Chapter Thirty-Seven

Paul sat Ernie on the floor outside the room and made him take deep breaths. He sent James to the lobby to wait for Johnson and stop guests from leaving or going upstairs. He photographed the room and corridor with his phone, then did a full video sweep from the doorway. He left Ernie's coffee pooling on the rug and told Lily to stay by the elevator. When Johnson and the cops came—real ones, not idiots in sportscoats—Paul did the talking. At the station, they separated her from him and Ernie and James.

"We meet again, Ms. Sparks," Johnson said.

"If you'd taken Vanessa Randall's death seriously, we wouldn't be here. And if your men hadn't wasted their time chatting up the piano player at The Brown—"

"Hey!" The paunchy detective threw up his hands. "That was your tip."

"And if you gave a shit about Angela Kurtz—"

"Look, Ms. Sparks." His jowls wagged. "I know you think we didn't—"

"—you'd do more than just go to the ICU to impound her clothes!"

Johnson poured them tar from a carafe with residue like low tide. She ignored hers. He saluted her with his mug. "Congratulations on catching George Kurtz's killer, by the way. How and why do you think his daughter's accident is connected to Ms. Randall's death?"

"Her shoes—" Shit.

"Which were missing as of yesterday," Johnson said. "But an ICU nurse saw you there with a dame old enough to be your mother. One of you stole them."

Leave Sasha out of it. "Why would I steal Angela's shoes?"

"You tell me!" His jowls quivered. "You're a lawyer—"

"Was."

"You know what happens to people who tamper with evidence. Can I see your purse?"

Lily stood. "You certainly may not!"

"Thought so." He motioned her to sit down. "Let's start at the beginning. Just how did you manage to be the person who found both dead girls?"

She repeated what happened, leaving out the fuck-me's and the gloves.

"And you think Ms. Kurtz was attacked because she was shoved on a crowded street?"

"Yes."

"Okay." He rose.

"That's it?"

"For now. We're processing the scene."

"What about Angela?" she demanded.

"People around you meet bad fates." He chuckled at the corny line. "Want me to tell you not to leave town?"

"I want you to find the killer!"

With Johnson's hand on her elbow, she allowed him to escort her to the door. Ernie and James were outside with Laird and Cam. Laird's ponytail was askew and Cam's eyes were red. Johnson had a long night ahead.

She turned to him. "I have a question."

"Anything, Ms. Sparks," he said wearily.

"What's Paul doing here?" she asked.

"He's a gentleman, he escorts his date to the police—"

"In Denver."

The hound-dog look. "Ask him."

"How was that Rockies game?" she asked.

His eyes widened like he'd been caught stealing a hotdog from a plate.

"Get some sleep, Ms. Sparks. Tomorrow's a busy day."

Chapter Thirty-Eight

It was 11:00 p.m. when they pulled up to Lily's condo.

"You're shivering." Paul took off his jacket and draped it over her shoulders like the kimono. She angrily shook it off. Nothing could erase Rachel's bulging eyes and puffy face, the piano wire holding her head to her body like a string.

"You haven't said a word in forty minutes," he said. She stared out the windshield. "If you want to blame someone, blame me."

Rachel had bitten her tongue so hard it bled. She could have stopped it or warned her. And what the fuck was Paul really doing in Denver?

"Say something, Lily."

She threw his jacket at him and reached for the car door.

"You're not going inside alone. For Christ's sake, Lily, talk!"

"Okay," she said, "let's talk. What happened at the Senate hearing?"

"Fuck."

"Surely not that."

"I ran into an old friend."

"And?" she demanded.

"He convinced me to leave D.C."

"Do I know him?"

"Nick Lang."

The nerdy engineer she let fuck her brains out in order to get over Paul?

"Can we go inside?" he said.

Chapter Thirty-Nine

The AC was on, and Jack was already curled up in bed. She fixed hot tea and settled in the chair across from Paul on the couch.

"If it's Nick, what does he want?" she said.

"You. Vanessa Randall was the bait... I held out on you. You deserve better."

"Nick's harmless," she insisted.

"You dumped him and I busted his face."

"But—" She didn't dump Nick, he'd disappeared.

"Men like him don't lose easily, Lily. But outside a prison yard, you don't often see a garotte."

"Garotte?" She was still trying to get her head around the killer being Nick.

"You need something to pull the ligature tight." Paul rubbed his eyes. "In India, robbers strangled travelers with silk hankies tied with coins. Now inmates make garrotes with wood for handles and wire from a broom, or ballpoint pens and a linen sheet."

Those grooves in Rachel's neck.

She shook her head stubbornly. "Nick's incapable of that."

"Because he's an engineer?" Paul snorted. "I'll give him this: the scrawny fuck has brains. He leaves the wire but take the grips so there's no DNA. And he's got balls. Offbeat was packed with people, and he could've been caught in the act. This time he cut it closer. He knew people would arrive at six, but garroting Rachel was slower and more deliberate than slitting Vanessa's throat."

But there'd been something almost tender in the way Rachel was posed. Unlike Vanessa, whose feet had been cruelly shoved into fuck-me's, the kimono felt protective—a solicitous gesture. Did he drape it over her shoulders because he thought she was cold? Or to distract her from what he was about to do? And the gold chain… "What was in her hand, Paul?"

"Johnson said a locket. Like teenage girls wear, a good luck charm." Or a gift. He shook his head with a sort of admiration. "Did you and Sasha really steal Angela's shoes?"

She wasn't about to incriminate Sasha. "But you were tailing Nick."

Paul rubbed his eyes again. "And he knew it. Bars, the gym—I thought he was waiting for me to make a move. So don't blame yourself for Rachel. This is on me, and I'm not taking any chances with you." He stretched and yawned, and she untied his shoes. Even in his socks, his feet were cold. She warmed them in her hands.

"You were pretty impressive at The Teatro tonight," she said.

"Too little, too late."

"More than Johnson—"

"Lay off him, Lily. He feels bad enough blowing Kurtz's case."

She tucked an afghan around him. Jack hopped up and settled within reach.

"I'm going back when it's over," Paul said. "To D.C."

"What about that boutique firm?"

"A fantasy." He laughed tiredly. "There's no place for me, Lily—not here, maybe not even D.C." He stroked Jack. "You'll be fine, you don't need me or your old man. You just need to get your game back."

Her lips grazed his cheek. Gray stubble, hint of sandalwood. The scar slept. "You didn't kill them, Paul."

"No? I might as well have."

"We'll talk in the morning."

"Yeah."

She tucked the afghan more securely around him and turned off the light.

Chapter Forty

She closed the bathroom door.

In the mirror over her sink she saw Rachel's face. Bulging eyes and bloody tongue—if she'd convinced Michel to cancel Hopper or Paul to take the killer more seriously, she'd be alive. She blinked, and Rachel's face was replaced by a more familiar image. Gritty and pasty and pinched.

Not tonight.

She scrubbed off what was left of her makeup. She should've told Johnson about Angela's fuck-me's. Stealing them was impulsive, but if they'd drawn the killer to Angela, they belonged in his hands. Now Paul was blaming himself.

She ran the water and waited for it to heat. They'd talk in the morning, but she'd never heard him sound defeated. That scar would always be between them—it, and her running out.

She peered in the mirror again. She looked like shit. Details please. Her gray showed. She'd canceled her touch-up to play games with Sasha. She'd have to text her so she wouldn't find out about Rachel on the news.... No wonder she couldn't see straight. Her eyes looked and felt like she hadn't slept in a week. They were bruised—not hers, or Rachel's.

They belonged to Alta Hilsdale, the Minnesota tease. No wonder Paul had finally had enough. Tired of waiting for the water in the sink to heat, she turned on the shower.

Get your game back, Paul had said. Too late for that, too.

Everything used to make such sense. Dad was infallible, a god she'd do anything to please. He'd cultivated her eye, made it their own little thing. Reduced the world to a set of data points that added up to patterns. *Details, please.* A game based on his rules. College, law school, becoming a lawyer—why stop playing when it worked? She turned the shower on full blast.

Paul had tipped the game board over.

He'd introduced her to paintings, made her question why she was practicing law. *Marvelous, isn't it*, he'd said, *to raise a daughter with the guts to leave something she's good at for something she actually cares about?* He believed in her—*You deserve more!*—but being a conservator had become a new game, with its own set of rules. She was always walking the line between artifice and art, and sometimes she didn't even know where the line was anymore. But nobody had made her hold out on Paul. *He* deserved more.

The shower was getting hot.

Paul deserved more, but that didn't mean the killer was Nick. Because she'd banged him? God knew she regretted their fling! Using him to try to exorcise Paul was stupid, but the affair had quickly burned out. And whatever was going on between him and Paul now, it just didn't add up to murder.

The mirror was steaming. Look at your own shit, her eyes said. Mom in the bungalow doorway—she'd wanted to leave, did it matter why? Now Angela and Rachel and Vanessa were gone, too. The killer had stopped the girl in *Hotel Room* from slipping the leash, but the story wasn't over. The gala was Friday. There was one more Hopper to go.

You're in the killer's head. Figure it out and beat him there.

She still had her eye. Details, please… What were details, but flaws? Tell-tale attempts to cover up.

Fuck-me's, gloves—expose her and cover her up. If the killer's grievance against women truly went back to Hopper, it must have started in Paris. Skinny Frenchmen with little beards and long shoes, concealing the goods but always getting the girl, men who didn't deserve what he was denied. Alta looking at him with contempt and fearing he hated her enough to throw her off a cliff. The cruel portrait of his mother. But Paul was right, Hopper never killed anyone. He must've come to some acceptance the killer couldn't. Did he paint it? That would enrage the killer most...

"Lily?"

She looked up and saw Paul.

"Jack woke me," he said. "We thought it was smoke—"

She pulled him to her and opened his shirt.

The scar was pink and tender, a pulsing lifeline to his heart.

Chapter Forty-One

Sunlight spins her honey hair to gold. In a sick version of *Room in New York*, the couple in the booth by the window lean into each other, touching even when they're not. Unlike the husband retreating to his newspaper, The Man ignores the menu. Instead of the omelets and pancakes for which this spot is known, he could eat a bowl of cement so long as she's across the table. Of course they don't see you. With the line waiting, and across the crowded floor, they only have eyes for each other.

"Mister?" the waitress says.

Instead of piano keys, Golden Girl's fingers graze The Man's cheek like she's seeing him for the first time and can't believe he's real. Last night she apparently got a lifetime's worth of sausage, but now she ravenously tears into her toast. How could you have been so wrong?

"What can I get you, hon?" The waitress's T-shirt has a logo of a sizzling egg.

You double down on her smile. She doesn't flinch, possibly thinks you're cool. Lucky for her, you're in no mood. "I'll have what they're having."

The waitress glances behind her, then taps her pencil on her pearly teeth.

"Who?" she asks.

"A joke, darlin'. Poached eggs and grapefruit juice."

"Toast or English muffin?"

"Muffin. Dry."

You must be in fighting form.

The waiter goes to their booth with coffee. They look up and smile, including him for an instant in their perfect little world. Eden before the fall.

The woman at the table next to you hee-haws. This side of the restaurant they pack 'em in like cattle. Her laughter pierces you like a knife, just like mom's used to. Another broken promise. The only way this turns out right is if you make it. Your head pounds but you mug for the waitress. She nods sympathetically.

"Tylenol?" she asks. In another lifetime, she could be The One.

"No, thanks."

"Right back with your eggs."

The Man—hell, call them by their names, after what they put you through! Paul attacks his omelet like it's raw steak. Lily butters another piece of toast and gives it to Paul—practically jams it down his throat. She laughs, a tinkling sound that somehow reaches across the floor. Your stomach churns. What else did she violate? Paul kisses her hand. He offers her a sausage—more fucking sausage!—and she gobbles it up. Get a *Hotel Room*!

"Here you go." Buttered muffin with jam.

Do you not know who you're fucking with? "Thanks, darlin'."

You scrape off the butter and jam and stab an egg. The yolk runs to the edge of the diner plate. You douse it with tabasco and regroup. Nick was a diversion, obviously a mistake. Paul suckered you into tailing him. And she fucked Paul despite the scar. Her betrayal is a shiv to the gut. They played you for a fool.

They will bow to me!

"More juice?" the waitress says.

"What?"

Does Lily want you to teach her, train her—correct her? Does she want you to get rid of Paul? She butters him a last piece of toast. The woman at the next table brays and brays and brays.

You're a fool. You're a fool. You're a fool.

You're unattractive, weak. Smash her face? She'll bow to me.

"Eggs cold?" The waitress makes a sad-clown face.

Paul and Lily are rising. They're making their way through the crowd at the door.

"I can bring more…"

Suddenly you're famished. You dump on the rest of the tabasco and swab up that beautiful red yolk.

"They're perfect."

Gut him in the locker room. Take her after.

Chapter Forty-Two

"There you are! Michel's been looking for you."

Lily turned from her computer, blocking the screen. "Later, Gina."

Gina was wringing her hands. "The Teatro was the last straw. The Whitney's pulling their loan, and the curator will only speak to you—"

"I said not now!"

Gina retreated.

"Poor Rachel," Sasha was saying on FaceTime. "*Hotel Room*, right? If Vanessa wasn't enough, she won't be either." Her TA Kate nodded sympathetically. It was noon on the last day of the Yale symposium, and they'd taken their box lunches to a quiet room. "Did you go back to the paintings?"

She'd spent all morning at the gallery. The gala's photo op was the killer's last shot.

"Think about his next step," Sasha prodded. "In *Hotel Room* she's studying a train schedule. Did she board the train? Even if Hopper let her—"

"—the killer didn't. We know that!"

Sasha nodded. "But is that where the story truly ends?"

She was right; to complete the woman's arc, there must be one more painting. But Michel's memo had been clear. *Mesdames et Messieurs: I am quite sure none of you will do anything to jeopardize the Hopper exhibition by revealing so much as a soupçon…* At the gala tomorrow night, the most warning she'd get would be a last-minute text from Ernie.

Kate was balling up the sandwich wrappers. "Don't forget the garrote."

Sasha wagged her finger at her TA. "Your generation's so cold-blooded."

But Kate was insistent. "Was there Chinese food?"

"At The Teatro?" Lily said. "Just Starbucks and a kimono."

"He left the wire. Maybe he left the grips too." Kate returned the wrappers to the catering boxes. "Was there a Chinese takeout carton?"

Sasha was as baffled as Lily.

"A garotte can be a cheese cutter or a clay sculpting tool," Kate said impatiently. She disappeared and returned with two plastic knives and a catering box ribbon. She tied the ends of the ribbon to the knives and pulled the ribbon taut. "Voilà!" Seeing their confusion, she made a scrolling gesture on her smartphone. "*Chop Suey,*" she said.

Sasha nodded. "Hopper, 1929."

Lily pulled up the painting of two flappers in cloches and tight sweaters with a pot of tea at a Chinese restaurant. Through the restaurant's window, a truncated neon Chop Suey sign read SUEX.

"Hopper's wink at eroticism—" Sasha began.

"—and what better way to wink at him, than use chopsticks for grips?" Kate said. Someone entered the screen and signaled it was time to go back. "If the killer's half as gamy as Hopper, he'd leave them at the scene."

Sasha smiled indulgently. "Grad students never cease to amaze." She waved brightly to Kate that she'd be right there. When she turned to Lily, her smile was gone. "But you have a perfect eye, and the ending's on the gallery wall. Go back and finish the story."

Chapter Forty-Three

"Chinese food?" Matt said. "A bit early for me."

Lily turned from the screen. Ernie had said her assistant was looking chipper. Matt's hair was different, now it had a cute little wave. What else had she been missing? Maybe Sasha was right, the answer was under her nose.

"Coming to the final walk-through?" Matt asked. The conservation staff was leaving for Gina's last instructional tour. He glanced over his shoulder at Willow, who was waiting. It wasn't just his hair; he seemed sleeker, more confident. Were they finally...? Willow had evidently chosen him over James. Was Hopper's woman's arc that linear?

Lily exited *Chop Suey* for *Girlie Show* and motioned to Matt.

"Yikes!" he cried.

"What do you see, Matt?"

He cleared his throat. "Interesting composition. Pillar, curtain, stage."

"The stripper," she prompted.

He blushed. "G-string, billowing drape, huge pointy..."

Taut nipples and toned legs warred with the black-rimmed eyes and scarlet lips that made the stripper's face so hard and old. If using Jo as the model was meant to make her ageless, *Girlie Show* was Dorian Gray's portrait on steroids and aging at different rates.

"And the men?" They seemed trapped between the edge of the canvas and the stage.

"Hopper just shows the backs of their heads," Matt said, "except that guy on drums." At a three-quarter angle, the drummer didn't bother to look. He'd caught the show before. Was the killer the drummer, or one of those faceless staring men? "Coming?" he asked again.

"Be right there."

He rushed to join Willow.

Sasha was right: the arc was incomplete.

Girlie was a sideshow, not where the woman's story ended.

—

"This late Hopper is an homage to America's post-war road trip," Gina was saying, "the highways through our nation's vast Western expanse, the generic new motor courts…" She and her staff were clustered at the painting of the woman in the western motel room.

Moving past them, Lily had the gallery to herself. She walked quickly through the gray and periwinkle rooms. In the mauve room, *Hotel Room* beckoned, but it was too late for Rachel and she hurried past. At *Couple near Poplars* she paused. Gloveless and with arms crossed, Gibson Girl shrunk from Beret Man's touch. Alta Hilsdale with the bruised eyes, who'd dreamt he wanted to throw her off a cliff? What happened in Paris hadn't stayed there.

She entered the next room.

Summer Evening's supplicating boy begged for a kiss, and the sullen girl stared down at her pastel-colored flats. Rachel and Bo had made it an entertaining riff, with the boy winning out. But Hopper's canvas was crueler. Skipping over the painting of the man at the Mobil station—a distraction, the wrong note—she moved to *Room in New York*. The woman at the piano draped her hand over the keys, her husband was engrossed in his newspaper.

Her footsteps echoing, Lily returned to *Summer Evening*. The boy still waited for the girl's kiss. She went back to *Room in New York*. The woman was still considering whether to strike a note. Back and forth she went between those two paintings. Like the woman poised to hit a key, the girl on the porch had all the power. The boy's frustration had hardened into the man's coldness, but the woman was out of reach to them both.

Heels clattering, she retraced her steps to the mauve room and forced herself to look.

Hotel Room was where the story changed. Not just for Rachel, but for the loose-limbed girl with copper hair. Like Hopper's other women, she looked down. Unlike them, she'd finally taken a step. Her bags were tagged and packed and standing upright on the floor. If she didn't catch that train, there would have been another.

Behind her, Gina coughed loudly. "Here we see—" she started to tell her group, but for once, even she was at a loss. "Now, the next painting…" They followed her to the man pumping Mobil gas. But where did the woman's journey end?

Lily turned to the painting of the elderly woman in furs gazing out the lobby window. Alone, maybe a widow—like Hopper's mother, Elizabeth Griffiths Smith, a postscript. But the climax to the woman's arc was still missing.

In the gray room, Kip and James were rubbing out floor marks from the war over the display case. "Big day," Matt said. He and Willow had sneaked out of Gina's tour. Lily followed them back to the entrance.

"Love the dress," Willow said, "but those shoes…"

Lily looked up.

Like the young wife's dress in *Room in New York*, *Western Motel* woman's was sleeveless and red. Befitting a more matronly Hopper woman, hers was wine-colored instead of scarlet, and her shoes were sleek black pumps. Her straight blonde hair was parted to the side and clasped behind her neck. But unlike his other women, her face and physique were completely in sync. She looked her age—she owned it. And she was looking straight at Lily.

Lily stepped back.

"Ms. Sparks?" Willow said. "I didn't mean to be flip…"

Like *Hotel Room*, this woman sat at the edge of a neatly made bed. Her bags, too, were packed and standing. This room was less cluttered and more spacious; the plush green art-deco armchair was replaced by a red one with a hard cushion and squared lines. The picture window framed a Western movie set: sun-tipped butte, green Buick, wide blue sky. The sky drew Lily's eye back to the chair. Instead of a kimono, something blue was draped over the arm.

Boxer shorts.

Lily looked from the shorts back to the woman. Like the shorts, the woman's hand was draped over the bed's footboard. Her middle and unadorned ring finger were crossed.

Gina and her entourage were leaving. Seeing Matt with Willow, Gina whispered to the Objects Conservator, who led Willow off. When the space around *Western Motel* was clear, Lily took a long last look.

Whoever the man was, the woman was leaving without him: his boxer shorts weren't packed. Outside the Buick waited, hood sleek and chrome bull's-eye signaling not just a flight to the future, but a clean getaway. Hopper's woman would be at the wheel. He'd finally let her go.

That was the ending the killer couldn't afford.

Chapter Forty-Four

Thursday afternoon the club empties early. Frackers and lawyers and day-traders spruce up for the brewpub or to get a head start on the weekend rush to the mountains. You're in no hurry. You have nothing to do but wait.

Hopper would love the men's locker room. A place to meet but not speak, look but not touch. Wood-paneled lockers, gleaming urinals, closeted toilets. Showers against the wall. Curtains end six inches from the tile floor. Drains slope; what happens in the shower stays there.

In the black tracksuit that makes you taller and hides your paunch, you sit on the bench and wait. Your gym bag is bright yellow, the perfect size and shape. You considered a club-branded one, but nobody notices you or remembers. *She'll love you for yourself,* that old monster promised, *when the right one comes along.* You practiced in the mirror. *Hi, I'm—* but you've given them all too many chances.

What's taking Paul so long? You've timed his laps. You could run a few yourself, put on some muscle, join a men's club or a single's dating group—not online, a real one. You tried that once before. Even got a dog. Soft silky fur, liquid eyes, snuffling black nose. But it didn't love you back.

The woman who took it promised to send it to a happier place. Was she The One? Forget Lily and Paul and the dog, go back to her, see if you can make her—

A gym rat enters and looks over at the bench. His Grateful Dead T-shirt's soaked, his sneakers reek, the space around the bench fills with treadmill sweat. He strips off the funky shirt and flexes in the mirror. He goes to a urinal, whips it out, and pisses. Ammonia replaces sweat.

Gym Rat looks over his shoulder. "Hey, dude."

Your hand tightens on the bag. Do you know what I can do?

Take him from behind, like Vanessa and Rachel and Angela and Nick. Put your knee against his back for leverage and garotte him with the wire while he's pissing. Drag him to a shower and prop him up so no one sees. Paul will be messier. She will be, too.

"Got deodorant, man?" Gym Rat asks.

You point to your ears like some slick invisible Bluetooth makes you deaf. You untie your sneakers and fiddle with a locker. Gym Rat gives himself a shake-shake-shake and heads to the showers. Paul's late. Good thing, too, with Gym Rat whistling away. Did Paul change at the pool deck? What if he meets someone he knows, or leaves without showering? So many decisions, so much mess!

You can't afford to wait.

You tie your sneakers and grab your bag. Paul won't recognize you— not immediately, not with his fogged goggles and itching eyes—but like a good FBI man he'll register your tracksuit, height and weight. If he's on the lookout, it'll be for Nick, who's taller and skinnier. Did they find Nick yet? You tipped them off, but you can't afford mistakes. You pull out your ball cap and cock it low. You exit the locker room and mount the stairs. If Gym Rat's there, you'll take them both. You stop at the landing.

You can have her without taking Paul.

Funny-looking kid, last to be picked for dodgeball. Never made a team, kissed by one girl. One day they'll bow to you—but when? Until now you've been invisible. Nobody ever buttered your goddamn toast.

Cologne wafts up the stairwell. Still whistling, Gym Rat takes the steps to the lobby two at a time. What do they have that you don't? Not a goddamn thing.

You have it all. Good job, esteem—*Whaddaya think, Hoppin' Mad?* You did everything right. You gave love one more chance with a girl you thought would understand. Did all you could to make her love you... Now you can be God. You open the heavy door to the pool deck. Chlorine and humidity envelop you like a sweaty glove.

Paul knifes through the water, oblivious to his fate. But a god can be merciful. Should you pardon Paul? He has nothing. No FBI, no job, no alibi for Nick. But he has her.

You picture what's coming. Paul climbing from the pool. Frowning from exertion, him striding past you downstairs to the locker room. While the shower heats he peels off his Lycra trunks. Unexpectedly modest for a guy so hung, he doesn't check himself out in the mirror. Or is he too self-conscious? That scar's an ugly motherfucker. How did he get it? Your eyes meet in the mirror. Suddenly he recognizes you. His eyes widen when he sees what's in your hands. He'll bow to me...

The water stills for real. Paul has finally finished his laps. He clambers onto the pool deck and coughs from the chlorine. He's tired and winded, his heart's probably thumping too fast. He wraps the towel around his hips. The scar writhes up his torso like an angry tapeworm itching to bust out. He squints and gives you a goofy grin. Last chance?

That fucking buttered toast. You unzip your bag.

"Hey, do I know you?" Paul looks past you. He opens his arms in a crazy kind of surrender. What would Hoppin' Mad do?

In this sweltering cesspool, his world collapsing, Paul looks... happy.

Cut off his balls and feed them to her.

You reach for Sweeney's razor.

Chapter Forty-Five

"You want me to close for a shopping spree?" Elena was already putting up the Closed sign and locking Brandt Fine Arts' door. "What if I miss a client?"

"He'll be back," Lily promised.

"Don't they need you for the gala?"

"Gina's territory." She helped Elena into the Prius. "But I need an outfit."

"Little late, isn't it?" Elena's own emerald off-the-shoulder shantung gown had been airing in her closet for a week, and she'd been wearing the Balenciaga pumps with crystals and sequins five minutes a day to break them in again. "Not like you to be spontaneous."

"Maybe it's time." She buckled Elena in and drove up Broadway.

"The mall's the other way," Elena said.

Lily drove past auto repair shops, tattoo parlors, and empty storefronts, searching for the place her hairdresser had told her about. It was noon but there was no foot traffic on this gentrifying industrial strip. If not for the Gatsby lookalike and fedoraed Marlene Dietrich mannequin in the window, she would have driven right past. She pulled to the curb.

Elena was aghast. "A transsexual thrift shop?"

"Vintage." The sign was red, with gold letters and black trim.

"You mean bordello," Elena said.

Inside, it was Central City taffy-and-souvenir shop meets Black Hawk gambling casino. Velvet Elvises on dark red walls were lit by a funky chandelier and floodlamps, glass cases featured buckles, feathered tiaras, and Bakelite bangles, and circular clothing racks were topped by boots and floppy hats. But this was no secondhand hodge-podge. The merchandise was arranged by color, era, and function and displayed to its best advantage. All Sales Final, a sign read.

"Elena, it's a museum!" Lily exclaimed.

"Salvation Army without the thrill of the hunt," Elena sniffed. "If you have to shop here, you need a raise." She frowned at some suede fringed jackets and corduroy sport coats, then moved to a rack of pearl-buttoned cowboy shirts.

"But look at the dresses, Elena. The tags even have waist and bust measurements!"

"The gala isn't a costume party," Elena said. "What exactly are you looking for?"

"I'll know it when I see it."

Elena rolled her eyes. Lily summoned the woman at the counter, whose smile and shrewd sizing up of her new customers marked her as the owner.

"1940s," Lily told her. "A red dress."

The owner led them to a rack near the dressing rooms. Rifling through it, she pulled out a scratchy cotton number with a ketchup-colored skirt and short-sleeved gingham bodice with red collar and trim. "Meatloaf special," Elena muttered.

"Dressier," Lily said. "Wine-red, low cut."

The owner's face came alive. "An evening tea swing dress!"

At the front of the store, tucked away by the cash register, a small rack held a handful of dresses. It was roped off with a sign requiring permission to shop or try the items on.

"Fabrics and age make them delicate," the owner said apologetically.

Each dress was exquisitely made. Princess-seamed bodices, cunning gathers and shirring, bias-cut skirts, side seams cleverly concealing zippers. The colors were saturated and the drape was soft.

"When women dressed like women," Elena murmured.

"Rayon?" Lily asked.

The owner nodded. "Big in the '40s." She gently flipped through the rack. "Here."

The sleeveless dress was deep red. With its sultry V-neck and mid-calf skirt, it seemed more suited to the wife at the piano in *Room in New York* than the matron in *Western Motel*.

"Want to try it on?" the owner asked.

The graft on Lily's forearm would show, but did she care? The dress was the right color and drape, and tonight more than her vanity was at stake. She looked at the measurements on the tag. The waist was right, but the bust was too large. Maybe she could pin the straps.

"No, I'll take it."

"About time you went sleeveless again," Elena said approvingly. "Do you have the right pumps?" She couldn't resist. "Black and matronly, like somebody's mother's?"

Lily turned to the owner. "Open toes."

"Sling-backs with ankle straps," she asked, "or peep-toe Mary Janes?"

"Burlesque, but not platforms," Lily said.

The owner nodded knowingly. "I can't guarantee the size." She hustled off.

"Fuck-me's will be ghastly with that dress!" Elena said. "What's gotten into you?"

"Nothing."

"You're positively…" Her eyes lit. "He's back, is he?"

"Who?"

Elena wrung her hands and looked up at the chandelier. "Thank God the cross-county madness is over!"

"For good." Like *Western Motel's* woman, Lily crossed her fingers.

The owner returned with a pair of fire-engine red fuck-me's two sizes too big. "Tighten the straps," she suggested.

And dye them blue.

Elena was getting into this. "I'll lend you my pumps just in case… Do you have black satin opera gloves?" she asked the owner. They scurried off like a pair of schoolgirls.

Lily checked her phone. Nothing from Paul. If she was wrong, she'd be a fool in bad shoes and a Big Band Era dress. If she was right… She texted him again. *Gala at 6.* Yesterday at breakfast he'd said he was going for a swim before drinks with the guys from the litigation boutique. Don't wait up, he'd said then. But he should've called by now.

Elena was back with gloves and a hairpin with inlaid crystals. "Costume," she whispered, "but a steal. Ready to go?"

The gloves reminded Lily. "Brown-leather ones?" she asked.

"Elbow length?" the owner said. Elena shuddered.

"No, the cheap kind with elastic at the wrist," Lily said.

"Best bet's a department store." She took their purchases to the counter.

"You're sure this is wise?" Elena asked Lily. "If I know you…"

"Paul and six hundred people will be there." The gala was sold out.

Elena shook her head. "Wear my pumps. They're easier to run in."

Chapter Forty-Six

Outside Brandt Fine Arts, Elena's best client paced.

"Put on your dancing shoes," Lily said. "He's ready to trot."

"Luck to us both." Elena checked her lipstick and pecked Lily on the cheek. "You're sure about those pumps?"

"I have what I need."

—

Lily drove to the shoemaker. Fred pushed his smudged glasses up on his forehead and looked at the fire-engine fuck-me's with fascination and revulsion.

"Where'd you find these, your granny's attic?" he asked.

"Can you dye them?"

"Before or after we resole them and replace the straps?"

"I'm only wearing them once," she said.

"They're not even your size, Lily. I can add a couple holes, but—"

"Come on, Fred. You've brought more than one masterpiece back from the dead."

He shook his head. "Even if we dye 'em, they'll just be fit for the dumpster. What color, black?"

"Peacock blue."

"Geez, Lily. They don't even make that color!"

She pointed to a small bottle of acrylic paint on the shelf. "Turquoise?"

"When do you need them?" he asked doubtfully.

"Today."

"Leather's like canvas, Lily." Fred was a true artist. "I have to prep 'em."

"I'll be back before you close."

—

She bought gloves at the mall and went to a makeup counter.

"You sure about that plum blush?" the pretty girl in the smock said. "It's not exactly flattering…"

"…for a woman my age."

"And the foundation is maybe a *touch*…"

"…pale."

She showed Lily lipsticks in soft pinks. Lily pointed to a deep carmine.

The girl leaned across the counter. "Can I be frank?"

"Sure."

"The point of makeup is to make you look better."

"Yeah?"

"That foundation washes you out, and the red's way too harsh."

"Wrap them. And the eyeshadow and concealer palette, please."

—

Her next stop was the florist.

"I need a bouquet for a friend."

The florist fluttered her long fingers and put on a mournful face. "In the hospital? We do a stunning arrangement of gladioli and roses."

"No! Something cheerful." Lily crossed her fingers again. "She's on the mend."

They settled on a bright assortment of peonies, snapdragons, and sweet peas.

"We can deliver them in the morning," the florist said.

"I'll take them now."

—

At the ICU, the charge nurse from her visit with Sasha was on duty. Hiding behind the bouquet, Lily waited for her to disappear in back and then plunked the vase on the counter and entered the ICU.

Angela was off the respirator but there was an oxygen canula in her nose. Her hands were still tied to the bedrails. Lily loosened the straps. Her fingers flexed—or did she imagine it? Maybe it was the oxygen, but she didn't seem quite so gray.

"It's Lily," she whispered. The lines on the monitor were waves gently washing ashore, but the canula twitched. She took Angela's stilettos from her purse and lined them up neatly under the bed. "You'll wear these again."

Angela's lids fluttered.

"I'll get him, I promise. Tonight's for you."

The monitor's tracings grew choppier.

"It was no accident, Angela—this goes way back. Is it Cam?"

Angela squeezed her hand. The waves rocked, and the monitor beeped.

"Am I right?" Lily asked.

Angela's lips twisted. She squeezed harder.

Lily leaned in. "Angela?"

Angela thrashed, pulling at the straps. The monitor beeped faster and louder. She gulped and exhaled loudly. The nurse burst in.

"What are you doing here?"

"Just—"

"Leave now!"

Angela's eyes flew open. Dilated, black, empty. Slowly they focused.

"Lily?" she croaked.

Two orderlies entered.

She clutched Lily's hand, pulling her closer.

"Get him."

Chapter Forty-Seven

Lily leaned into her bathroom mirror.

The killer's first sight of her tonight was crucial. From what distance and under what lighting would she be viewed? Dutch Golden Age Masters meant their paintings to be viewed under candlelight; a candle's flicker and glow were impossible to replicate in a modern gallery or conservation lab. Now she was the artist.

She stepped back.

There was a science to the optimal distance at which a picture should be seen. From inches away, an image was unreadable, but at a distance, details and form took shape. Michelangelo knew that proportions that were off from cubits away were perfect at meters. But she wasn't painting the Sistene Chapel. She was trying to gauge the effect of her grand entrance on the killer.

Ping! Paul?

She grabbed her phone. A text from Sasha. *Good luck 2nite.*

Where was Paul? He swam to psych up, to be in top form. Being late must be good news. Would that firm make him an offer?

She returned to the mirror.

The gala would be warmly lit to flatter the guests. The track lights over her sink were warm, too. She was working under the right lighting to create the impression she wanted to make on the killer. But from what vantage would that be?

She pictured her arrival.

Ushered through the portal in the *Nighthawks* screen, guests would find themselves in the anteroom where *Western Motel* was displayed. Then they'd be shuttled through the partitioned rooms.... But that would come later. First, at the entrance, would be hors d'oeuvres. The killer had probably been in Offbeat's lobby reveling in the excitement when Vanessa was found. Tonight, he'd be mingling with guests at the wine and food, soaking in the anticipation. She could amp up the drama by arriving late—but not *too* late—and slowly ascending the stairs. The challenge was shrinking the distance between the bottom of the grand staircase and the gallery's entrance to the space between her mirror and wall. To create the impression she wanted at that distance, she had to make her features older and more stark.

She looked dispassionately in the mirror.

Skin thinned with age, especially around the eyes. Like oil paint, the lids became transparent, revealing uneven reds, purples, and blues. Hopper had begun that progression in his unsparing depiction of Alta Hilsdale in her youth and brought it brutally home in the portrait of his elderly mother.

Lily frowned. Fine lines at her mouth deepened.

She smiled. The crinkles around her eyes became a web of cracks.

Good.

Light blonde brows, silver threads at her temples and crown. Skin smooth but fragile. Freckles and tiny age spots. Small pores, no pocks or draws. Full lower lip. Thin upper which almost disappeared. Walking the line between art and artifice, she'd wiped centuries off Artemesia Gentileschi's gentlelady through painstaking cleaning and skilled restorative strokes. Now she'd do a reverse Gentileschi on herself.

Lily scrubbed her face with hot water and bath soap. Deprived of its natural oils, her skin instantly tightened and shrank. To rough it up more, she rubbed her face briskly with a towel.

Ping! Sasha. *Chop suey any1?* Lily silenced her phone.

She set out her new cosmetics on the bathroom counter alongside her old brushes and tools. Instead of doing her eyes first to avoid shadow and mascara flecking onto powder, she started with foundation. The pale department store stuff—more was more. Rather than blending towards her ears, hairline and neck with her fluffy flat brush, she vigorously stroked it in with the smaller one designed for concealer.

Brows were making a comeback, but she skipped her usual darkening mousse and thickening gel. Without them, her features were strangely naked and undefined. Did she really want to look this bad for Paul? Like any competent restoration, this was reversible, of course, but the ghost of Christmas future might not be so easy to erase. On the counter her phone jiggled. Him? She grabbed it.

Another text from Sasha. *Garrote?*

Paul's department—he'd figure it out. He'd be there tonight, he never let her down. She tossed the phone on her bed and returned to the mirror.

Should she go dewy? She dabbed Vaseline under her eyes, over her cheekbones, and across the bridge of her nose. Too uniform and shiny, like a heavy varnish. She was going for an older, more mature look. The Gentileschi—herself but more so.

She wiped off the Vaseline and doubled down on shimmer powder. Like the hapless restorer who'd overloaded the Gentileschi with gray pigment which only made its deficits more pronounced, the powder accentuated her wrinkles. Its weight drew her lips into a Hopper-esque frown and darkened the purple around her eyes to bruises like Alta's.

Now she turned to her new cosmetics. In the eyeshadow and concealer palette, circles of paint spanned the color wheel. The Impressionists had mastered color theory. Monet and Degas's blue-violet shadows highlighted orange-red sunlight; green canceled red. To darken the circles under her eyes, she dabbed on pink. This was kind of fun. She stood back.

She looked ill.

Lily reached for a Q-tip, a younger cousin to the wooden sticks she'd wound with cotton to clean the Gentileschi. When she tried to rub away the pink, the delicate bags under her eyes puffed up in protest. Cotton balls with cold water calmed things down. She began again with a fresh Q-tip moistened with her own saliva. The first time Matt saw her spit on a swab he'd been aghast, but the enzymes broke down grime. If it was good enough for the Gentileschi… Last traces of pink gone, she gently applied a neutral concealer, then the unflattering plum eyeshadow and blush.

She looked twenty years older.

Now the lips. Her signature shade was a creamy rose, but she painted on a thick coat of carmine. She blotted and applied a second coat.

Five p.m. Where was Paul?

Thirty minutes till Fred closed.

Lily took off her robe and went to her closet. Ignoring the shiny scar on her arm, she slipped the vintage rayon dress over her head and zipped it up the side. Her kingdom for bigger boobs! Pinning the shoulders ruined the drape, and the bodice still gaped.

She rummaged through scarves and jewelry. Not the right look. Frantically she searched her lingerie drawer. Lots of lace, nothing padded, no push-ups. Even her power bra fell short. She couldn't just stuff it with toilet paper like in middle school. Strapping on a second bra made her feel like Heidi climbing the Swiss Alps in all her dresses and coats…

College dorm—that old trick.

She found a safety pin. Clipping her bra straps together in back turned it into a racerback. She slipped the dress back on and zipped it. Yowzah! Her cleavage was impressive and the safety pin didn't show. Add to permanent repertoire.

At the back of her closet were her old black pumps. They added two inches to her height and tilted her pelvis forward. She took a couple of practice steps. Her stride shortened, and her hips swayed. She parted her hair on the side and pulled it severely back from her face.

The woman in *Western Motel*?

Lily pictured her now, in her low-cut red cocktail dress and sleek pumps, perched at the edge of the neatly made bed. Shoulders squared, facing the viewer defiantly but with fingers crossed. Not a stripper, whore, or shop girl bent over coffee in an automat at night, nor a woman in a bleak hotel room pondering which train to catch. Autonomous, on the move—free at last! The killer couldn't let her go. He'd punish the bitch who dared look back.

Lily stood once more in her full-length mirror. A chill ran up her spine.

She was her mother.

Chapter Forty-Eight

In the atrium lobby, Holly, bespectacled and with a green lanyard, turned disappointed visitors away. Friday nights at the museum were normally dead, with tourists opting for downtown gallery walks that offered wine and cheese to wash down the cultural experience. But tonight was the gala.

"Ms... Sparks?" she said.

"Hi, Holly. Quite a crowd!"

Patrons streamed through the doors. Holly smoothed the feathers of one elderly gent who hadn't seen or read the *Closed For Private Event* sign by giving him and his wife a weekday pass to non-ticketed events. She waved in a man wearing a Van Gogh tie and cummerbund and his date in a slinky cocktail dress. She turned back to Lily and peered at her strangely.

"Something wrong?" Lily said. Foundation, or eyes?

"Just... what a cool dress!"

Lily gazed up at the atrium. At the second-floor balcony, patrons were milling around with wine glasses. In the alcove, a swing band played. Tonight the atrium's magnificent staircase seemed pharaonically wide, or more suited to Aztecs hurling virgins to their doom than ushering guests to a blockbuster event. Maybe it was her pumps. The heels reminded her why they'd landed in the back of her closet; they were difficult enough to navigate in without worrying whether the safety pin in her bra would hold. Adjusting her straps with a toss of her shoulders, she slowly climbed the stairs.

"Lily!" Gina's short taffeta dress was iridescent green, and her black satin stilettos' laces were tied in an extravagant bow behind her skinny ankles. She was with a bored-looking older guy in a tux whom she did not introduce. She gave Lily an air kiss, far enough away not to disturb each other's makeup or knock them off balance. "Where's your FBI man?"

He was never late. Was his new firm already exacting its pound of flesh?

"He'll be here."

Gina frowned. "You look tired." She leaned closer. "And your dress—"

Recognize it?

"—I know a good stylist," she whispered.

Elena stood at the top of the stairs with a flute of champagne. Her dress was the same shade as Gina's, but on her it looked good. Two local male artists were on her arm; despite razor-thin margins in a down economy, running a gallery still offered some perks. Elena pecked one of the artists on the cheek and drew Lily aside.

"Good lord! Is that flour on your face?"

"It washes off."

"It better." Elena waved to the owner of the state's largest petroleum company. Her ticket to the gala would be a tax write-off, and she was scrupulous about earning her deductions. She stepped back. "Whatever you've done to your bosom, keep doing it." Laird Bennett was talking to the governor and his new young wife in a ballgown and cowboy boots. "She's from back East," Elena stage-whispered, "she wore a Stetson in her first-lady portrait." After a failed bid at the White House, the governor was looking at the Senate. "Word is, she's pushing him to bid sky-high on Gina's photo op because she wants to use it for her inaugural."

Cam was at the hors d'oeuvres. Tonight *Western Motel's* woman would hijack his riff. She imagined confronting him at their own private photo op. *Who was the first girl to turn from your teeth, Cam? Was it Angela, or did you push her into that SUV because of her fuck-me's? What's your plan now—take me from behind too?*

Laird was staring at her. Like a conductor's baton, he waved his cheese straw at her. Kate's cheese-cutter... Forget the garotte! But where was Paul?

Her arm itched. Without sleeves, she felt naked.

Laird liked them old? Hah!

Ping. Paul?

Kate. *Broom straws?*

When this was over, she'd send Kate a blood-red pair of chopsticks, and Sasha size five peacock-blue fuck-me's. But now she was starting to worry about Paul. How much trouble could he get into over drinks with lawyers?

Michel's scrum was coming her way. A woman in a tiara squeezed his hand. "Angela would be so pleased!"

Michel nodded excitedly, then froze. Was it meant as praise, or a condolence? Americans were so—effusive and insincere. Ambiguous. A charming shrug was always best. "Yes, our poor dear Angela..."

Across the floor, Cam was helping himself to a top-heavy cracker. He said something to the waitress, who immediately turned away. Crazy to think he'd reveal himself in front of six hundred people. If her new get-up passed his test, he'd try to get her alone.

Gina's assistant was running around with a top hat and slips of paper for last-minute bids for the photo op. Her boss had been vindicated. Instead of making patrons squeamish, the frisson over the murders was adding to the bidding frenzy. When the auction closed, they'd start shepherding patrons through the gallery. The winner would be notified and dolled up to pose.

Lily looked down at the lobby, trying to spot Paul. Rachel being garotted at The Teatro hadn't fazed him one bit. So calm and focused—

she could use some of that now!—he'd known exactly what to do. He'd secured the scene and put James to work ensuring nobody entered the hotel or left. From the doorway he'd photographed every inch of the room and videotaped it so no detail was lost. He'd even shot the table in the hallway outside the door. He'd be wasted at that boutique firm....

The jazz band was getting louder. The crowd was growing, pinning her to the balcony. The perfume and cologne on the couple next to her made it hard to breathe. What code inspector ever thought this many people in such a small area would be hygienic, much less safe? The band was deafening. Behind her, waiters circulated hurriedly with final flutes of champagne.

Focus.

The killer was gamy. He'd taken the razor he'd used on Vanessa but had left the wire from Rachel's garotte. Did he leave the grips? If only she could see Paul's footage! But whatever he'd shot, she'd seen too, in the instants before and after Ernie screamed.

Details, please.

She closed her eyes and pictured the room. Not Rachel, the objects. Coat, cloche, flowered kimono. Bureau, bed, chair. Valise, suitcase. The locket—not a weapon, whatever it meant. Pumps with diagonal straps kicked off on the rug—

"Last call for bids!" Gina's assistant cried.

A harried server came by, and the man with the cologne grabbed a drink from a tray. Half a flute of cold champagne splashed onto Lily's bosom.

"Shit!" Was she a magnet for every slob with a wine glass? At least this time her dress was red. The server rolled his eyes sympathetically and gave her a cocktail napkin. She turned for privacy and dabbed her chest. If it was the worst that happened tonight, she'd be lucky.

Suddenly her plan seemed not just stupid, but crazy. Cam was still at the hors d'oeuvres, and Laird was talking to the petroleum entrepreneur. No one had his phone out to ping and lure her to another location. Nobody was even looking at her. When Paul came, they'd get out of here and grab dinner. He could tell her all about—

Champagne was soaking into the rug.

Where the hell was Paul?

Focus.

Hotel room. Valise and suitcase. Shoes kicked off. Except for the locket and Rachel dead in that kimono, it was Hopper's painting. What didn't belong?

She looked at the champagne on the floor.

Iced lattes. Cardboard tray and plastic cups.

Lids popping off. Ice cubes flying, coffee soaking into the rug. What Offbeat didn't buy, it scrounged. Thick black plastic straws, a matched set. Strong, pliant, easy to grip—strong enough not to bend under the wire of a garotte.

Her phone pinged.

Chapter Forty-Nine

"Give me my phone," Paul demanded.

"Hot date?" Johnson said.

"Fuck you. It's been twenty-four hours." His Lycra swim trunks chafed under his gym clothes, which they'd allowed him to don before hauling him in. When he saw cops at the side of the pool, he'd raised his arms because he thought it was a joke. There was some guy with a gym bag, too—he didn't get a good look because by the time he took off his goggles the guy had scurried away as if being busted was infectious. If this fiasco ended in diaper rash or crotch rot, it'd be the least of his indignities.

"How long is a hold in D.C.?" Johnson mused. "You can have a lawyer—oh, I forgot! You are one. By the way, I did tell those stuffed shirts you planned to meet that you were unavoidably detained."

"Prick." Forget that boutique firm making him an offer.

"I warned you to stay away from Nick Lang."

"Message received. Can I go now?"

"Tell me again how you happened to be on The East's surveillance cameras."

They'd been over it countless times, but he was obviously being taught a lesson. Johnson kept fingering a manila folder. Maybe he did need a lawyer.

"I was looking for a short-term rental—"

"Directly opposite Lang's?" Johnson asked.

"That was the display model."

"Does it also explain why you were surveilling him?"

"It was the perfect night for al fresco Thai." Give The East credit for a fisheye lens that had obviously caught him on the park bench.

Johnson's stubby thumb worried the folder's edge. "Leasing manager said you're in Denver for a patent trial. I didn't know the FBI did that kind of work."

"He got it wrong."

"He get your name wrong too, Mr. Custer?" Johnson was itching to show him that folder.

Paul leaned back and folded his arms over his chest. "Lying to a rental agent isn't a crime. And I'm sure I'm not the only one who hates Nick Lang. Now will you tell me what happened to him?"

Johnson slid the folder across the desk.

The first photo was a color close-up of Nick's bulging, blackened face.

The second was a color close-up of his throat.

The third was a black-and-white of him on the slab. It looked like he'd been dead a couple of days. A cleaning person would notice the smell.

"Ligature?" Paul asked.

Johnson pursed his lips. "You tell me."

"Where'd you find him?"

"Townhouse."

"When?" Paul demanded.

"Yesterday at noon."

"How?"

Johnson shifted in his chair. "We got a call."

That fisheye pointed away from Nick's door, which meant they didn't have the killer on tape. "Who found him, a cleaning person?"

"The call was anonymous." Johnson finally had the grace to look away.

"You think I killed him and called it in?"

"Stranger things happen."

"Strange?" Paul's feet hit the floor. "This is fucking insane! Johnson, you know me..."

"Enough to know you have zero self-control or common sense when it comes to that little art conservator!" Johnson took off his glasses and rubbed his eyes. "You had a hard-on for Lang because he was banging her. He was in D.C. two days before he was killed. Then you show up in Denver. That's some coincidence."

"I didn't say it was." Who was doing this to him?

"Think it's a frame job?" Johnson gave a short laugh. "First Lang, now a stranger—how many enemies do you have?"

Maybe it wasn't about him.

Paul looked again at the close-up of Nick's throat. Two horizontal lines cut into his swollen neck. One had a faint braided pattern. There were no scratches or claw marks on the skin. He passed the photo back. "Nick was attacked from behind with a nylon clothesline. Think he'd let me do that?"

Johnson peered at the photo.

"Same MO as the two actresses," Paul continued. "Surprise attack from behind, to the throat—no defensive wounds or chance to cry out. How many of those do you see in a week?"

Johnson rubbed his eyes again.

"But you're right about one thing," Paul said. "I'm not the target."

"Yeah?"

"I'm just in the way."

Johnson gave him back his phone. Lily's last text was *Gala at 6.* It had been underway for nearly an hour. No time to stop at The Westin and change. Johnson gave him a jacket. Plaid, and the arms were short.

"I'd lend you trousers—"

"This coat's bad enough."

"Smells better than you," Johnson retorted.

"Let's just saddle up and go."

Chapter Fifty

The text was from Ernie. *Sneak preview.*

Lily looked up. The bidding had closed. Gina and her assistant were herding patrons through *Nighthawk's* imaginary door. Ignoring the counterman in the white jacket and peaked hat, they pushed on through. From across the floor Ernie waved.

She texted Paul. *Get here now.*

No reply.

Ernie pointed to the door to the back corridor. At its end, it accessed the gallery.

On the arm of the petroleum magnate's matronly wife, Laird saluted Lily sardonically. Cramming down a last pâté-laden cracker, Cam was right behind him. Elena waved gaily. Michel followed her in.

Ernie held up his hand with fingers spread. Meet me in five.

Lily nodded. He wanted an audience, did he?

Stall till Paul got there. She leaned over the balcony, willing him to rush through the door. Holly was locking up behind the last guests. Shrugging helplessly at Ernie, Lily went to the ladies' room.

The governor's wife was at the sink. "Better hurry," she told Lily, "or you'll miss the announcement of the winner." She lowered her voice confidentially. "The hubby made a preemptive bid."

"Don't go," Lily said.

"What?"

Keep her here with you. "The photo op—"

"—will be a fab portrait!"

Or her last.

Lily thought fast. "They'll make you ditch the boots and wear a retro dress like mine."

"Really?" She smiled uncertainly, then winked. "We'll see."

Lily grabbed her arm. "Tell them you'll pose tomorrow."

She looked at Lily pityingly. "It won't be news then." She dried her hands and left.

Lily removed her pumps and put them in her purse. She slipped on the fuck-me's. Fred had done a good job; the turquoise had a pearly sheen, and he'd punched new holes in the straps. She looked in the mirror. The blonde was no longer a stranger. She was the flapper and the woman at the piano and the girl with the train schedule. The ones who'd tried to slip the leash.

Cower here or make him face you. This was her only chance to stop him.

He wanted an audience of one.

Her.

Chapter Fifty-One

Lily entered the back corridor with her key card. In the gallery on the other side of the wall, guests oohed and aahed. Tickets sold to the public were timed at fifteen-minute intervals to comply with safety codes and keep up the pace, but tonight patrons would linger over centerpieces like *Summer Evening* and *Room in New York*. At *Hotel Room* there'd be whispers. Isn't that the one where that poor girl...?

The sounds grew fainter. At the end of the partitioned rooms lay whatever mock-up of *Western Motel* Ernie had staged for the photo op. Michel would milk the suspense by waiting until the last possible moment to announce the winner. The governor's wife would have to be convinced to surrender her boots.

Ernie. That aw-gee Kewpie-doll bobblehead, the gap in his teeth. The razor, the straws—keeping her from The Teatro until it was too late! Cam was pathetic, but he cared about Angela. How could she have thought the killer was him? And what would her riff be now? *What did those poor actresses do, Ernie, mess up your sets?*

Teetering on the fuck-me's and clutching her purse, Lily reached the door at the end of the corridor. Like the alcove at Offbeat, it was unlocked. If she could go back… She turned the knob, half expecting to see Vanessa.

She gasped.

Unlike columns in a park to evoke a porch, or period furniture to simulate a Depression Era hotel room, Ernie and Kip had created a full-sized replica of *Western Motel*. In this airless room, sealed off from the world, Hopper's 1950's tribute to the hospitality industry had been fully rendered and brought to a queasy kind of life.

The walls were avocado, the curtains orange. The artificial light was cold but bright; the goosenecked bedside lamps were strictly props. The burgundy bedspread was faded by a relentless fake sun streaming through the picture window, which opened onto yet another set—a painted western landscape. The only thing that looked real were the leather valises on the floor at the foot of the bed. Soft and dented, neatly tagged and packed, they pointed resolutely to the door. Just two things were missing: the woman, and the man whose blue boxer shorts were folded on the armchair.

Behind Lily something stirred. But she couldn't tear her eyes away. The more she looked, the more disoriented she was. Through the window a barren mesa slumbered like a sprung sofa, deeply shadowed but top-lit by the sun. She couldn't tell the season or time of day. Entombed in the museum, Hopper's static artificiality was compounded by the total absence of natural light.

Focus on the car.

The Aztec green 1954 Buick had bug-eyed headlights. Its grill grinned like a shark—expectant, alive. Hopper wouldn't let Jo drive it, but like the owner of those blue boxer shorts, he wasn't here. Now the Buick and Hopper's woman had places to go.

A moist breath caressed Lily's shoulder. She turned.

"Bullseye Bomb Sight. Wicked, eh?" James pointed at the hood's foot-long chrome ornament. It blasted through a cylindrical sphere like a gladiator's spear or a torpedo from a marauding wolf pack.

James?

He gestured to the window. "Plate glass, not plexi like Gina wanted. She's so cheap—and who knew Kip was such a purist? You should see the look on your face." Cold light gleamed off his balding head. "What, you expected Ernie? That little fuss-budget's busy kissing up to Kip and Gina for a job. I had him text you to make sure you came."

The straws. Set designers weren't the only ones who scrounged; art handlers were resourceful too. Whose idea had it been to go to Starbuck's for those lattes? But Kip and Ernie and hundreds of people were on the other side of the wall.

James laughed. "Know what I like about museums? The acoustics are shit. Even if the gawkers shut the fuck up, no one will hear you. And don't expect your FBI guy to come."

Paul.

He'd be calm. At The Teatro, instead of drinking his latte, he'd set it and the straws on the table outside the door. Even before Rachel was found, did he instinctively know how those straws had been used? She eased closer to the door, but James blocked her way. He was stocky, like a wrestler, but he'd taken his victims from behind. She had to keep him in front of her. Find his ground zero and make a break for it. The riff…

But he wasn't Cam or Ernie, he was James. And he was staring at the fuck-me's.

"They don't belong," he said. Not what a woman—*his*—was supposed to wear.

"With this dress?" she asked.

"On you, at all." He pointed to her purse. "Put on the pumps."

She opened her purse and pulled out the brown-leather gloves instead. Gina had had to remind him to wear gloves to transport *Couple near Poplars*, but he'd forced them onto Vanessa's hands. "You left yours on the piano. Did Angela offend you by calling them tacky?"

His lips twisted. "That braying bitch! She's one to talk, prancing in those shoes."

The riff, the riff… He'd brought Willow soda with lime at Sasha's reception, had left Rachel holding a locket. Gifts.

"She didn't deserve it," Lily said.

"What?"

"The locket. Who was she, James?"

He licked his lips. "Three guesses."

"Not Angela—or Rachel or Vanessa." This wound was deeper, and far older.

"I'll count them as one." His smile was scarier than his rage. Who hurt him, how could she know?

"Alta," she said.

James's smile vanished and he reared back in surprise.

"Or maybe the girl in *Summer Evening*, in that sexy bandeau and shorts," she continued. "You were on that porch, weren't you, James? But why the kimono and gloves?"

"To cover them up." Expose her with the fuck-me's, cover her with the gloves. How could he let them leave? If he couldn't have them, no one would.

James had maneuvered her to the bed. His fists were clenched, but if he had the ingenuity to use Starbuck's straws as garrote, he could stash a weapon anywhere. She glanced at the door.

"Not coming," James said.

"He will."

"Damn, that was an ugly scar! Like a fish out of water, on a hung guy like him." He laughed. "I gutted him at the pool."

"You're lying!"

"Yeah?" He said it pityingly.

Paul was dead. How else would he know about the swim and the scar?

James reached behind the pillow and pulled out a razor.

Sweeney's? Fuck the props.

Weapon? She had one.

"Put on the pumps," he ordered.

Trembling, Lily perched at the side of the bed by the window. Willing her hands to be steady, she slipped off the fuck-me's and put on the pumps. Slowly she drew back her shoulders and crossed her legs. Aligning herself with the front end of the Buick, she draped a hand on the bed's footboard. Damned if she'd let him stage her death. She'd be ground zero. The woman who looked back.

She took a deep breath and stared the fucker who killed Paul straight in the eye.

"Whatcha got, Jimmy?" she said. She made her voice throaty, huskier—older than Rachel's Valley Girl and deeper than the wife's at the piano. "Another cheap gold locket?"

He stopped.

"Still waiting for the right one to come along?" She gave a jeering laugh. "Or will you take me from behind, like the others?"

He stared at her, mesmerized.

"Try getting rid of that paunch, then worry about handling a real babe."

"Bitch!"

"Let it rip, Jimmy. Show me what you got."

"Why, you—"

"Come on, little boy." Her rage peaked. "Get me."

James lunged across the bed. Lily pulled to the side and raised her hands. As he hit the window, she shoved as hard as she could and let his momentum do the rest.

"From Angela and Paul!"

James had no time to scream. Like a rogue wave crashing ashore, he flew face-first through the shattering glass. The Buick's Bullseye Bomb Sight found its target.

Dead-center in his shiny balding head.

Chapter Fifty-Two

"Nice blouse," Paul said.

Lily smiled and squeezed his hand. He'd bought it for her. It was late August, way past the time to go sleeveless. Dad sat across from them in the booth. "Since when do you eat steak with eggs?" she asked him, but he was too busy sopping up yolk with the buttered toast Paul gave him to answer.

"Since he's been going to breakfast with me," Paul said.

Dad looked up and grinned. "Fooled you, didn't we? Some perfect eye." He'd lost an incisor he was too stubborn to replace, but with the weight he'd put on since he and Paul had been palling around, he was in fighting form. Even Jack seemed feistier.

"Easy on the tabasco, Harry," Paul cautioned. "You know what it does to you."

The litigation firm was still in the running, but he had his FBI pension and enough savings to hint about buying a house. Wasn't her condo good enough? Her phone rang, and she went to a quieter corner of the restaurant to take Angela's call.

"Still on for lunch?" Angela said.

"Liquid, I assume… not broth or tea?"

"Martinis!" Angela cackled. "Doctor's orders. I feel like Godzilla in these orthopedic shoes." She wasn't quite steady on her feet, but after lunch they'd go shopping for more stylish flats.

A blonde woman and her little girl rose from the booth by the door. The girl giggled as the woman bent to dab sunscreen on her face. She put some money on the table and took her daughter's hand. They walked out of the restaurant together. Lily wasn't wondering anymore about why her mother left. The ghost in her memory had gone with the woman at *Western Motel*.

A burst of laughter came from her booth. Dad must have told a joke because Paul was practically rolling on the floor. "What'd I miss?" she asked them.

"Guy talk," Paul said.

They laughed again.

So much had happened.

Cops had swarmed the gala, and the governor had credited Lily for saving his wife from the crazed killer at what would have been her photo op. James's death had closed the actresses' cases, but it had been hell convincing the Hopper lenders not to pull their loans. Even from her ICU bed, Angela dictated the terms. In the end, Michel considered it a point of pride for the show to go on, and the museum's patrons wholeheartedly agreed.

Hopper had broken the Van Gogh exhibition's records. Even with extra hours, it had been extended two weeks to meet demand. Now it was going on the road to sold-out crowds.

The day after the show closed in Denver, Lily had handed in her resignation. For the first time ever, Michel was speechless.

"What's your next move, Lily?" Dad said.

She smiled. "We'll see."

Acknowledgments

I am deeply indebted to *Automat's* eagle-eyed editors, Mark Chimsky and Janette Macdonald. I am also grateful to Victoria Becker and Jane Stein, my partners in crime. Most of all, I thank my husband and best friend, John, without whose love and support I would never set pen to page.

Edward Hopper led a fascinating life. Alta Hilsdale's letters to him are collected in *My Dear Mr. Hopper*, edited and with an introduction by Elizabeth Thompson Colleary. For more about the artist's life and work, read *Edward Hopper: An Intimate Biography*, by Gail Levin.

About the Author

Stephanie Kane is a lawyer and award-winning crime novelist. She has lectured on money laundering and white-collar crime in Eastern Europe and given workshops throughout the U.S. on writing technique. She lives in Denver with her husband and two black cats.

For more information, please visit *www.writerkane.com*.

If you enjoyed *Automat*, please post a review. Reviews help books reach new readers!